WHO AM I?

"Mary Elouise, I bet I look strange to you with my long dresses, and my short Afro. I used to have thick, straight hair down to my waist," said Miz Imani, "and I was so proud of it that I'd stay at the beauty shop for hours getting every kind of thing done to make it straighter, just like in the pictures in *Ebony* magazine and *Essence* and on TV."

"Oh lucky!" I said.

She shook her head, and her big earrings jangled. "But at the same time I got to be so vain about it that I was mean to my friends. I bragged about how much money I spent trying to get it so straight that it would blow in the air. I was so involved with my hair that I wouldn't take time to play baseball or dance or go bike riding or anything. Didn't want to get that fine hair dirty or messy or kinky one little bit, you understand. Sometimes I even pretended I had blond hair, blue eyes, and real light skin."

What? She did that, too? I didn't think anybody did that but me. I wanted to ask her why she used to feel that way. I know why I do.

"This sounds just like you, Mary Elouise," said Hattie.

"Oh, it doesn't!" I said quickly. But my face was burning, and I knew it was true.

SEP 08

CH

Other books you will enjoy
Ask your bookseller for the books you have missed

DON'T SPLIT THE POLE: TALES OF
DOWN-HOME FOLK WISDOM, Eleanora E. Tate

A BLESSING IN DISGUISE, Eleanora E. Tate

THE SECRET OF GUMBO GROVE,
Eleanora E. Tate

FRONT PORCH STORIES AT THE ONE-ROOM
SCHOOL, Eleanora E. Tate

THE WILD MUSTANG, Joanna Campbell

SONG OF THE TREES, Mildred Taylor

MAIZON AT BLUE HILL, Jacqueline Woodson

MOVING MAMA TO TOWN,
Ronder Thomas Young

FOLLOW THE LEADER, Vicki Winslow

ELEANORA E. TATE

THANK YOU, DR. MARTIN LUTHER KING, JR.!

A YEARLING BOOK

Published by
Bantam Doubleday Dell Books for Young Readers
a division of
Bantam Doubleday Dell Publishing Group, Inc.
1540 Broadway
New York, New York 10036

ISBN: 0-440-41407-5

Reprinted by arrangement with Franklin Watts
Printed in the United States of America
January 1997
10   9

To Tabitha Foster, Tequila Thomas,
Shequila Bradley, Lisa Steinberg,
and to grandmothers everywhere.
You are all heroines, too.

THANK YOU, DR. MARTIN LUTHER KING, JR.!

CHAPTER

ONE

I knew the answer, but I wasn't saying. Friday, January 15, didn't mean diddly squat to me. I glanced at my mouse pin, the same kind that Brandy Howard wore. I'd sure be glad when Social Studies was over. Then maybe I'd get a chance to talk to her about us wearing the same sort of jewelry.

"Friday, my little sugar plums!" our teacher, Miz Vereen, said. She waved her arms in the air like she thought we sat way across some field. She did that a lot. I liked her. I could tell she liked me, too. She asked me to help her do stuff lots of times. "Why is Friday important?"

" 'Cause it's somebody's birthday, I bet," hollered Hattie Stackhouse, my best friend. She sat in the back of the room by Brandy. Lucky!

Miz Vereen cocked her head to one side and pointed her finger up in the air. "Yes, it's a birthday, but whose?"

"My dad's," said Bubba Todd. "He's thirty-four."

"How sweet! But that's not the whose I meant," Miz Vereen said.

Hurry up, recess. I glanced around at Brandy again. She had long, pretty, blonde hair, blue eyes, a real deep tan, and talked like somebody from "Barbie's Adventures" on TV. She moved here from San Francisco in November. She lives in Cypress Swamp Cove, where the really sharp condos are. Her momma drives a lime green Mercedes, and her daddy is a retired Air Force colonel. Kids say she has a $50-a-week allowance. All the boys swear they're in love with her, and just about all the girls want to be her best friend.

Especially me. I'd made up my mind about that this very Wednesday morning while Miz Vereen collected our milk money. Brandy and I hadn't really talked to each other yet, but we would! And then that'd be the start of something—something totally awesome. I hummed to myself, thinking about it.

"Is it your birthday, Miz Vereen?" asked Buffy Perkins.

"No, my dear," said Miz Vereen. "Think hard, children!"

Kenyatta Threadgill, another new girl in our class, raised her hand. She moved here from Florida about the same time Brandy got here. Kenyatta is a Black girl with real dark skin. I don't like real dark skin, not even mine. It doesn't seem as pretty as pink or light brown, at least not to me. She wears long, skinny black braids with beads. Her name is funny-sounding, too, like it's foreign. I don't know any foreign Black kids. Kenyatta said she was born in Miami, though, so I guess she isn't.

I wear my hair pressed and in a ponytail, but I wish I had a Jeri curl like Libby Burns has, or real long, blonde hair like Brandy's.

I wish my skin was the same kind of pinkish tan color that Brandy's is, too—or even light brown, like Libby's. Mine is as dark as Kenyatta's. I wish my nose and lips weren't so big, either. Big Momma calls this old black mole on my cheek a beauty mark, but shoot, to me it looks like a wart. Big Momma tells me all the time to be proud of what I got, but I don't figure I have much to be proud of. I guess I don't see what she sees.

"Miz Vereen, I know!" Kenyatta was saying. "Dr. Martin Luther King!"

"You are perfectly correct," said Miz Vereen, nodding her brown curly head. "And exactly who was Martin Luther King? We've talked about him before, haven't we?"

I scooched down in my seat a couple inches.

Right here things usually got embarrassing. Miz Vereen could say some awfully weird things about Black people. Right now she looked like she was wound up to say some more. I wished nobody ever said anything about US, good or bad, not in school or on TV or NOWHERE.

"He made it so Black people could vote, I think," said Ernie Spurlock. "He got shot, too."

"Dr. King was a Negro minister who wanted to help his people progress. He was known all over the world." When Miz Vereen smiled at me, I looked down at my desk. "Friday's his birthday, and next Monday, the third Monday in January, has been named a federal holiday in his name. I don't see why they couldn't have made General Robert E. Lee's birthday a federal holiday, too, but they haven't."

When she stopped, I straightened up in relief and looked at her again. So far, so good.

"I'm going to show you something about Dr. King. Wait, I told you, didn't I, that I was born and grew up here in Calvary County, then moved away?" She picked up a bundle of *Gumbo Grove Gazette* Kids Pages sheets, and handed some to me. I helped her to pass them out. We all said yes, she had already told us. Didn't matter. She had to tell us again. She liked to talk about how she used to teach at a big fine school over in Horry County. I sat back down.

"But I got so homesick for these parts that I just had to come back and teach at this nice school. Of course, the teachers here do things differently from what I'm used to. I—Now, where was I? Oh yes, Dr. King. Dear children, please read the story about Dr. King on page three. Remember what I told you about Negroes not having all of their rights because they'd been slaves?"

I scooched down again, and my face got hot. There she went! Why'd she bring up slavery so fast?

"You said they came over here from Africa in chains, too," said Carrot Causey. "They didn't wear a stitch of clothes, their hair stuck out all over their heads like Buckwheat, and they had bones in their noses."

When Bubba, behind me, kicked my chair and laughed, I jerked around. My cheeks felt like they were on fire, I was so ashamed. "Stop, you!"

"Stop? Me? Why?" Miz Vereen looked at me puzzled. "Mary Elouise, all of you here who are our wonderful Negro Americans should be proud of what your people have done to rise from such lowly beginnings."

She smiled so wide I could see her gums. I didn't quite know what "lowly beginnings" meant, but it didn't sound nice. I didn't like her when she talked like that, either. I wished I had some sulfur or some turpentine. I'd put some around her desk, like how Big Momma sprinkles it around her house for snakes. She said it locks up their jaws so they couldn't bite. Maybe it would lock up Miz Vereen's so she couldn't talk.

"No-o-o-o, Miz Vereen, not at my house," said Pooch Walterboro. "Nobody in my family ever ran around naked or had bones in their noses."

"Libby Burns's family did," Hattie giggled.

Everybody burst out laughing. That was an awful thing for Hattie to say. I had to grin, though, too, but behind my hand.

I wasn't sure I wanted to read that sheet Miz Vereen gave me. Sometimes what Miz Vereen passed out in school for us to read was embarrassing to me, too. Seemed like she found only shameful, old-timey stuff about my people to make us read. I glanced across the words out of the corner of my eye. Seemed okay this time.

Recess finally arrived. I hopped from my seat and hurried to the front of the row. Good luck: I managed to get right behind Brandy. We trooped out into the hall and lined up at the water fountain.

While Brandy talked with Ashley Gustafson, I watched and listened closely. I loved how Brandy hung her head to one side when she talked. I got up my courage.

"Brandy, what do you want to be in the Presidents Month play?" I asked with my head slanted over, too. "Like, I want to be—like, like, narrator, okay?"

When she didn't say anything, I tapped her on the shoulder. "Brandy, when you—"

"What, what, what?" She swung around and her hair flew in my face.

"Brandy, look, we got the same kinds of animal pins, see? Brandy, when you—"

"Yeah." She glanced at my pin, then turned back around.

Brandy Howard talked to me! While she talked again with Ashley, I gathered up some strands of her hair. It hung down from the thick, fluffy, pale yellow ponytail perched on top of her head. She had also wound red scarves around another clump of hair sticking out on the side of her head above her ear. She was so sharp! I began to braid a few strands of hair, hoping she would say something else to me.

"Eeek! Omigod, like there's a geek in my hair!" Brandy pulled her hair out of my fingers, and hurried up the hallway with Ashley.

I hopped over to Hattie. "I was just talking with Brandy!" I waited for Hattie to be impressed and say so, but she didn't.

"She even called me a geek," I said proudly.

Hattie shook her head. "You don't even know

what 'geek' means. It means stupid or dumb, like a nerd."

"Oh." My face burned. I thought it meant I was sharp. "Anyway, we were talking about the Presidents Month play, and our pins." I let out a long sigh. "Don't you just love her hair? It's soo soft! Wish mine was long and pretty like that."

"Mary Elouise, would you please!" Libby lisped beside me. I saw the rubber bands stretch around her braces in her mouth as she talked. "It looks like a pile of hay and rags to me, the way she's got it tied up with fifty eleven thousand rubber bands and strings and mess."

Then Libby glared at Hattie. Hattie waggled her head at Libby. I knew they were getting ready for another fight. They fought a lot, then they'd make up, and then they'd get into it again.

Hattie moved over by the glassed-in display of the seashell collection and put on her jacket. Libby put her hands on her hips. "But even hay looks better and prettier than what that ole ugly Black thing Hattie calls hair," she said loudly. "Her and her bald head."

Chaundra Finkley laughed. Well, when she laughs, she screams, you know? And when she screams, everybody stops what they're doing to see what's up. Which is what everybody in the hall did just then.

She screamed again. "Hattie, Libby called you ole ugly Black thing!"

Timika Bellamy and I shook our heads at each other. But Bubba, Carrot, Ernie, Pooch and Jamal Gore let out whoops of laughter.

Hattie's face balled up like a wrinkled old prune. She held out her hand, palm side down. She stuck out her little finger and forefinger, balled up her other fingers, then held her hand like that under her nostrils. She looked like she had brown bones sticking out of her nose. "Bone-in-the-nose!"

This time all the kids—Kimiko Johnson, Timika, even ME!—broke out laughing.

Libby stuck her long, yellow nose up in the air. With one hand she patted her long, Jeri-curled hair. "Ole ugly thing! Baldie!"

Giggling, we pushed in close around them. Hattie wiggled her fingers under her nose, then stuck her nose and hand in the air. "Elephant legs! Bone-in-the-nose!"

"Ole ugly—"

"Shame on you!"

Miz Stokes, a white fourth-grade teacher, pushed in between us. Her face was red and her brows were frowned together something awful. "You girls ought to be ashamed of yourselves. You don't go around low-rating each other like that!"

She took Hattie and Libby each by an arm. "Don't let me ever hear you talking like that again, do you hear?" She leaned down over Hattie. "I said, 'do you hear?' "

"Yes m'am," she said. Her face was wrinkled up now worse than a ball of aluminum foil.

Miz Stokes leaned down over Libby, who had her lower lip stuck out so far she could have walked on it. "And what do you say?"

Libby whispered "yes m'am," too.

Miz Stokes looked up and glared at me. When I saw what looked like fire jumping out of her blue eyes, I got frozen with fear. "And don't any of you ever talk that way, either. Have respect for yourselves, do you hear?"

We mumbled "yes m'am." Miz Stokes spun around and stomped back up the hall to where Miz Thomas, a Black fourth-grade teacher, stood. Then Miz Nisby, our librarian, who is Black, and Miz Smith, the Black third-grade teacher, came along. They all started to talk and point at us. Those were all the Black teachers in the whole school Miz Stokes was telling that stuff to! Boy, were we in trouble now!

"C'mon!" Hattie hissed. We flew outside to the sidewalk. Pepper Holloman, Chaundra, me, and some other kids crowded around Hattie. Kenyatta, Timika Bellamy, and some others crowded around Libby.

"Boy, I thought Miz Stokes was gonna bite you guys' heads off," said Chaundra with another scream.

"Girl, shut up!" said Hattie. "I didn't even hear Libby cracking on me until you and your big old mouth had to repeat what she said. I sure hope Miz Thomas and them don't tell Momma."

"It'd serve you right if she did, and told Libby's Aunt Eva Dell, too. You guys talked nasty," I told Hattie.

Kenyatta came over and started up a game of jump rope with Pepper and Chaundra. "My mom said we shouldn't ever make fun of what other people look like," she said, bouncing up and down between the ropes.

"Yeah, but, Kenyatta, you gotta admit that Libby does look like an elephant, with that long nose and those fat legs," said Pepper. She loved to tease folks.

Hattie added some more choice words about Libby.

"You all better stop before some teacher hears you again," I said.

"Well, Libby didn't have any business calling me names." Hattie kicked at the sidewalk.

"Libby said you started it," Chaundra told her, "back in class."

"But I was just joking. I didn't say a word about nobody's color or hair."

I stood around for a few minutes and listened to them fuss. "Well, play tryouts are tomorrow," I finally said. "What parts do you all want? Brandy and I were talking, and she—"

"None of 'em." Pepper jumped into the rope as Kenyatta jumped out. "Just give me the cake, candy, and the Valentine's party," she said. "Nobody likes the Presidents Month play, anyway. You gotta be George Washington or Lincoln or their wives, and you gotta memorize a bunch of dull stuff or sing dumb songs."

"Shoot, I'd try out if there was a good part," Hattie said. "Somebody interesting, like Whitney Houston or Janet Jackson."

Everybody went, "Yeahhh!"

"Well, Brandy and I were—"

"Brandy and you weren't, either," said Pepper. She poked Hattie in the ribs with her elbow. "I saw you trotting after her all the way to the water fountain, jabbering at her so much the girl couldn't even get a drink."

"She did, too, talk to me!"

Sometimes I think there must be two Mary Elouises. There's me—the Mary Outside—who does things normal. Then there's this Mary Elouise who sits inside my head and says things I would never dare say out loud. I call that one Mary Inside.

Mary Inside said, Pepper's trying to make them think you're fibbin'.

"She did, and I ain't fibbin', neither," I said.

"Nobody said you were," Pepper said back. "Well, you might have been holding a conversation with *her,* but it sure didn't sound like she was holding any kind of conversation with *you!*"

Chaundra screamed out again. She and Pepper slapped hands.

"Quit it, you guys," Kenyatta said. She smiled at me, but I didn't smile back. Brandy talks to Kenyatta a lot. I think Kenyatta wants to be friends with Brandy, too. I wish Brandy would talk more to me.

"C'mon," said Hattie to me. "Let's go over to the basketball court and see what the guys are doing."

We walked across the dry brown grass to the court, and watched Pooch and Jamal clunk heads trying to catch the basketball. After a while I said, "Pepper's just jealous cause Brandy's talking to me and not her."

"Why're you so fired up over Brandy?" said Hattie. "You act like you and her are best friends or something. You got Brandy on the brain."

I kept quiet. I couldn't tell her that I wanted Brandy to be my best friend, too. Then we could do everything together at school. And of course she'd invite me to her parties and sleepovers. She'd had three sleepovers already, but she'd invited only her special friends Buffy and Ashley from our class. They were the other two most popular girls in the whole fourth grade. Hattie said Kenyatta was pretty and real popular, too, but Kenyatta didn't count to me the way white girls did.

So if I could be Brandy's best friend, then I'd really be IN. And I'd be just like her and Buffy and Ashley—popular, just like the white girls were.

CHAPTER

TWO

When the final school bell buzzed, I grabbed up my book bag and crammed my papers in it, ready to fly to the door. If Miz Vereen called on Brandy's row to leave first and my row next, I could stand right behind Brandy again. Brandy sat in the last seat in her row, see, and I was first in mine. Maybe we could talk again.

"Quit, boy!" Pooch yelled, and hit Bubba over the head with his spelling book. "Miz Vereen, Bubba punched me!"

Well, they made my row be last again. Brandy was gone before I could get up from my desk.

Outside in the cool January air, Lonnie Lee and Bonnie Boo Woodard and I pushed each other, screamed, and laughed. Steam rose from the cars and buses waiting in the curved driveway. Lonnie Lee and Bonnie Boo hopped onto Bus Number Two and waved good-bye to me.

Miz Cutterhorn and Miz Stokes, who were on duty, clapped their hands for order. "Don't run out into the driveway like that, girls!" Miz Cutterhorn yelled.

I saw Miz Howard's Mercedes pull away from the curb with Brandy, Buffy, and Ashley. I wished I could have been in there with them, too.

I waited around for Hattie and her younger sister Maizell, but I didn't see them. I didn't see my friend Timika, either. I usually walked home with her when I couldn't find Hattie or my seven-year-old little brothers Antoine and Andrew. Just then I heard a peck at the window behind me. When I looked around I saw Timika inside her classroom looking out at me with a sad face.

I ran over to the window. "Come on!" I shouted.

"Can't. We gotta stay after, the whole class, for half an hour."

"How come?"

"This lady from the electric company came to talk to us this afternoon about conserving energy or something. She was awful boring, so nobody listened. Miz Stokes got mad. Here she comes, too. I gotta go. See ya."

I didn't mind walking home by myself. The sun was bright and it wasn't freezing cold out. Freezing cold only lasts a few days in January or February here in Gumbo Grove because we're right by the Atlantic Ocean, in South Carolina. One day it'll be twenty degrees and the next day it'll be seventy.

Gumbo Grove is like a resort, but not like Six Flags or Disney World. We've got amusement parks, beachwear stores, malls, video arcades, putt-putt golf courses, regular golf courses, and Gumbo Grove Air Force Base.

Folks like to come down here and splash around in the water, but I won't go in *nobody's* ocean. There's sharks, jellyfish, worms, and crabs out there that'll eat your toes off, and the rest of you, too! Me, I prefer a swimming pool. I was in one once.

A lot of kids whose folks are stationed at the Air Force base go to Gumbo Grove Elementary School with me. They come from all over the place. Kimiko Johnson is Japanese, from California, like Brandy. She lived in Japan for a while, she said, before she moved to California. Alicia Valendez is Hispanic, but she isn't from Spain or Mexico. She's from Arkansas and Texas. There are some kids from Vietnam and Thailand, too. Oh, and there's Kenyatta, from Florida. Her father is a pilot and her mother is a doctor at the base. Her momma drives a shiny white Seville. I still don't really like Kenyatta, though.

I counted the change in my pocket. I had just enough to buy something to eat on the way home today and maybe tomorrow. I stopped into McDonald's at the mall and bought a bag of French fries. When I came out, I saw a million seagulls standing one-legged in the parking lot, waiting for somebody to throw them some food. Pretending to be a seagull, I threw a French fry in the air, and opened my mouth to catch it.

"Awgfgh!"

A seagull flapped right up in my face and snatched the French fry practically out of my mouth. I threw my arms up in front of my face and almost threw my bag of French fries away. "Get gone, crazy thing!" Boy, I cut down the street away from there!

The birds made me think of Libby and her long yellow nose that looks like a long yellow beak. She had a lot of nerve calling Hattie names. But if Libby told her Aunt Eva Dell, her aunt would call up Hattie's momma and bawl her out. Then Hattie's momma would bawl out Hattie. Miss Eva Dell had a lot of pull, Momma said, being assistant superintendent of schools here.

One time Libby told her aunt that George Dozier threw her new coat in the mud. Miss Eva

Dell told Miz T, our principal. Her real name is Thessalonia Hawthorne, but she lets us call her Miz T. Anyway, Miz T told George's parents to get the coat cleaned. They took the dry cleaning money out of George's allowance to do it. The awful thing about it was that George wasn't the one who got her coat muddy. Libby dropped it in the mud herself on a dare from Bubba! Most of the fourth grade is afraid of Libby. Course, Hattie isn't. Hattie isn't scared of anything.

I turned onto Fifteenth Street—Hattie and a lot of other kids live on Fifteenth, too—and carefully walked around the mud puddle on the dirt path past the Gumbo Limbo Soda Fountain and Cafe. We all like to hang out there when there isn't anything else to do.

Libby Burns doesn't hang out at the Gumbo Limbo, though, and she doesn't live on Fifteenth Street. She lives on Seventeenth, in a two-story tan brick house with a big grassy yard that Miss Eva Dell won't let a soul step on. She even chases the cats and dogs away. One time in Sunday School I heard Miss Eva Dell call Fifteenth Street the lower-class end. Libby turned right around and told Hattie that Fifteenth Street was the lower-class end, too. Hattie waited until Sunday School ended. Then she popped Libby upside her head hard with her fist and dared her to holler.

Libby has money, too, but not as much as

Brandy has. I heard that Kenyatta's folks have a lot of money, too. Well, I'm going to be richer than all of them one of these days. I have it planned out. By the time I'm sixteen I'm going to be a famous actress like Kim Fields, or be a rock star like Whitney Houston. I'm nine now, so I have seven more years to get my stuff together. I practice singing and acting a lot already. At home after school when I'm by myself I watch "Barbie's Adventures" and lip sync their songs.

I don't get to practice every day because lots of times I have to clean the house or do the washing. Or Andrew and Antoine want to watch "The Transformers," "The Hulk," or "Mr. Ed," which all come on about the same time as my show. You know who usually wins: them! My sister Argentina hardly ever comes right home after school. She likes to hang out with her girlfriends. The only TV shows she likes are "Soul Train" and "Bill Cosby."

I bet Brandy doesn't have to do the laundry. I bet she doesn't have any brothers or sisters to clean up after, either. Cypress Swamp Cove Golf Course, where she lives, has bunches of fancy condos and villas and houses almost a block long. I like to imagine that I live there. I could just see myself lying on my fancy bed in my fancy blue-and-white bedroom talking to her on my very own private telephone, doing our homework together.

Or I'd be lying on her fancy bed in her fancy

bedroom, which I hear is done in peach. We'd do our homework together. Then we'd get in her swimming pool—or mine—drink cherry colas, or play tennis.

When I saw Momma leaning inside the trunk of our old yellow Pinto parked in our driveway I quit daydreaming. "Mary Elouise, come help me with these sacks," she called when she spied me.

I took a sack. "Can I watch TV for a while before I have to do homework?"

"No m'am. You march yourself right to your bed and study those books." She puffed in sideways through the door with three bulging sacks, and set the sacks down on the kitchen table. Pulling her handkerchief from inside her coat sleeve, she wiped her hands. "I've got to go back to work and fill in for Essie Lee until eight or nine at the hotel. Where's Argentina?"

"I don't know."

"Well, when you see her, tell her to heat up that macaroni and cheese and the chicken. If she's not home by five-thirty, you do it. Tell Antoine and Andrew to clean up that mess they made under the carport. I'm late already. Mary Elouise, would you put up the food, turn the washing machine on, and do that load in the blue basket?"

"Yes m'am." I wished Argentina would come home and help me, but I knew she wouldn't slide in anytime soon. And even if she did, she'd get on the telephone and gossip for hours with her girlfriends Raisin or Bunny or Big Boy. Raisin is Hattie's big sister. Bunny is Pooch's big sister. Big Boy, who is a girl, doesn't have any brothers or sisters.

When I pulled out a package of cookies from the sack, my stomach growled, and Momma heard it. "Oh my lands sake, please eat something quick! Get yourself a few cookies and some iced tea, too. Eat at the table, and clean up after yourself. How was it at school, all right?"

She went back out to the car and brought in two brown blankets and some girls' clothes. She'd got the blankets from the hotel; her boss gave them to us a lot. I figured she'd got the clothes from there, too, left in a room. I hope I can get that yellow jumper she held; it was cute. I don't mind wearing secondhand clothes. Lots of kids do it. You can get some neat stuff from clothes that tourists leave in the rooms or give away. And almost everybody's folks work in hotels, restaurants, or beachwear shops—some own one. One time Ernie came to school wearing a T-shirt with a picture of a motorcycle on it upside down. He said his dad made a mistake printing up a T-shirt for a customer, so he gave it to him.

After I finished putting up the food, I turned on the washing machine and headed for Argentina's and my room. As soon as I heard Momma pull out of the driveway, I flew back to the kitchen and grabbed up two more cookies. If I didn't get them now, the boys would eat them all up the minute they got home.

I plopped on the couch in the living room, munching. With the remote control, I flipped on the TV. Today I'd find out what happened to Barbie, Tammie, and Pammie, the three girls who star on "Barbie's Adventures." They get into all kinds of trouble, and travel around in a rock band. They wear the latest clothes, are rich, and have bunches of boyfriends. Tammie has long, red hair; Pammie has long, brown curly hair; and Barbie has straight, blonde hair that hangs down her back, just like Brandy's does sometimes.

In this last adventure, the president of the United States had given them some important documents that a foreign secret agent wanted. When the agent found out that Barbie, Tammie, and Pammie had the documents, he decided to chase them. In the last episode I saw, their private plane had run out of gas. They had to make an emergency landing on the freeway, then they hid in the woods.

When the show came on they were still in the woods. Hopping from behind one tree to another, Barbie, Tammie, and Pammie danced and sang and shook their hair. Suddenly they all had their instruments and microphones. A stage appeared from nowhere. They sang, banged on drums, and flipped their guitars. I settled my dolls on the couch like they were my audience. I have four dolls that I still like to mess around with. Their names are Pixie, Bam Bam, Poopsie, and Caroline. They all have blonde hair, blue eyes, and real-life, soft skin. Big Momma gave them to me.

Snatching up the remote control—my microphone—I lip-synched with the TV set. I had an idea! I pulled the yellow cover off the couch pillow and tried to fit the open end on my head like it was a stocking. It slipped off. "We're the finest in the land," I sang, rummaging through Momma's desk. I finally found a big safety pin, and pinned the extra cloth around my head. The rest of it hung down my back.

There! I danced and sang around the living room, thumbing my guitar hard, singing into my microphone. I was Louisa, famous rock star! Shaking my beautiful, long, blonde hair!

The show ended. I pulled the pillowcase off my head, thinking about Brandy. Momma was always after me to be friends with important people. And to do that, she said I had to have things in common with them. Well, I heard Miz Vereen say Brandy would be perfect as Martha Washington. If I got a part in the Presidents Month Play, too—an important enough part—we'd have something else in common. And be closer to being friends! I had to grin about that.

Of course, Pepper was right about the Presidents Month play being dull. But it was better than being in no play at all. I flopped down on my bed and opened my speller. If I got an important part, it'd be a first, though. I never got any parts in plays. I sang in the chorus every Christmas, every Easter, in every spring program, and in every Thanksgiving program. Always in the back row. I wondered if I could get one of the narrator parts in the Presidents Month Play.

Maybe I could hint to Hattie about how much I want one of those parts. Maybe she'd put in a good word or two for me to Miz Vereen.

CHAPTER

THREE

The next day the other fourth-graders were already in the cafeteria by the time my class got there to try out for the play. We held our plays and programs in the cafeteria. It had a stage at one end. My class was always the last to get anywhere. Half the time it was because of Pooch and Bubba. The other half was because of Miz Vereen, who didn't like to walk fast, not even for something important. We always had to walk like proper little ladies and gentlemen.

"All the parts are gonna be gone by the time we sit down," said Lonnie Lee in front of me.

"Yeah, every one," said Bonnie Boo. Her real middle name is Bea, but she likes "Boo." Lonnie Lee and Bonnie Boo are white girls, twins, and two of my good friends. The same things happen to them. They fall down, scrape knees, break arms, have nose bleeds, and get the flu at the same time. They both have thin, pixy faces, eyes as gray and round as a kitten's, and short brown hair. They make the same grades I do, too—B's and C's.

When Miz Riley, our music teacher, gossiped with the fourth-grade teachers—Miz Vereen, Miz Stokes, Miz Cutterhorn, and Miz Thomas—I leaned over toward Brandy in front of me. "Hi Brandy," I said.

She turned around and stared at me, finally said "hi," then turned back around.

She must have felt my fingers coming. Just as I reached out to touch her hair, she jumped around. "And don't touch my hair ever again, okay?"

I giggled. When she said "okay" through her nose, it sounded neat. "But it's so soft and pretty," I said.

"Yes, I know." She combed her fingers through her ponytail bunched and tied up on her head with red, purple, yellow, and blue scarves. She plumped at the rest of it hanging on her neck.

Hey, we were talking!

Miz Riley interrupted our conversation. "Children, we're ready to begin working on this year's Presidents Month play." A couple of boys behind us booed, but she acted like she didn't hear them. "We're going to emphasize the roles our presidents played with the U.S. Constitution and our country's laws."

More kids booed. Some groaned. This time our teachers snapped and pointed fingers at us in warning.

I hoped Libby didn't get a big part. When she got to be the chief elf in the Christmas play, you'd have thought she'd been chosen to play Santa Claus himself!

Miz Riley went on. "We're also going to emphasize the fact that February is the month of love and Valentines. And don't we all love to be loved? And get hugs and kisses?" She fluttered her eyes behind her sequined eyeglasses and clasped her hands to her chest. We all laughed. I like Miz Riley, too.

"We're adding a special observance of Black History, too," she said. "Because Dr. King's birthday is a holiday now, we feel we should honor him, along with some of our other famous Black Americans."

What? I got tight inside. Why'd she have to put THAT stuff in our play? She'd never done it before!

"What's the matter? Don't you like love and Valentines?" Lonnie Lee asked me. "Your face is pinched up worse than Silly Putty."

"Nothing." I don't figure that she'd understand if I told her. Nobody would, except maybe Hattie.

Miz Riley read off parts—for George Washington, Miz Washington, Abraham Lincoln, Miz Lincoln, James Madison, Miz Madison, John Adams, Thomas Jefferson, for a Valentine's skit with a Cupid and a puppy who became friends with a kitten, and for three narrators.

"That skit sounds weird," Lonnie Lee said. "We've got a kitten and a puppy, but all they ever do is fight and eat each other's food."

"Yeah," said Bonnie Boo, "and scratch."

When Miz Riley talked about Black History parts I stopped listening. I tuned back in when she came to the music parts. "There's plenty of great songs for you to sing. We'll have a full chorus to sing 'Battle Hymn of the Republic' and 'Over the Rainbow,' a choral reading of a special rap, and a reading of James Weldon Johnson's 'Lift Every Voice' poem."

She stopped and studied her sheet. "And it says here 'Swing Low, Sweet Chariot.' We'll also need a drummer, a piccolo player, a flag bearer, and, unh, field hands."

She called off names so we could try out for the different roles. First she called names for the part of Martha Washington. One name was Brandy's, of course. Now came names for possible parts in the Valentine skit, and Black History. When she called mine for possible narrator, I jumped right up in relief.

The kids trying out for the Presidents segment followed Miz Stokes and Miz Cutterhorn over to one corner of the cafeteria. The quartets, choral groups, and rappers followed Miz Riley over to another. By the time Miz Vereen reached us, Miz Thomas had us already settled down at the tables in the narrator, Valentine skit, and Black History corner. Miz Vereen carefully sat down, crossed her legs, and adjusted the bow around her curly brown hair.

"Sugar dumplings, the Valentine skit must be ver-r-r-ry romantic, so you must be ver-r-r-ry dramatic." Miz Vereen waved her arms around. Imitating Miz Vereen, the kids in the skit waved their arms, hit each other, giggled, and read their parts.

The boy who was Cupid turned red when Miz Vereen showed him the suit he'd wear. The top was white with red wings. The bottom was red tights with little white hearts going up and down the legs and on the behind. He was supposed to carry a bow and arrow, too.

"How're you gonna shoot a sponge arrow out of a sponge bow?" Pooch asked him.

Aaron Griggs got the puppy part, and Kasheba Skipper got the kitten part. They'd wear dog and cat suits that would cover them from head to toe, except for little eye holes. Some girl from Miz Stokes's class got the part of a big white bone with a blue ribbon wrapped around it. That was the kitten's Valentine present to the puppy. A boy from Miz Thomas's class was a big orange ball of yarn, the present the puppy was to give to the kitten.

"Now we'll work on the parts in the Black History section," said Miz Thomas.

"I hope she doesn't call my name," I told Alicia.

"Why not?" said Miz Thomas, who had ears like bat radar. "Don't you want to be in the play?"

I nodded yes, but I looked down at the floor. How could I say to her, "But not in *this* section?"

When Miz Thomas held up a picture of a Black man with wavy hair going every which way, my face got hot.

"Whooo, that dude needs a haircut," said Pooch. Some of the kids laughed, but I didn't. "Was he a president, Miz Thomas?"

Miz Thomas called Pooch by his real name— Cleavonne—which Pooch hates. "Cleavonne, mind your manners. No, he wasn't a president, but he was just as important as any president. Children, this man's name is Frederick Douglass. He spoke out against slavery. He was for women's rights, too. Cleavonne, how about you trying out for him? Step up here and read the part."

People started to laugh and groan. Most of us in Miz Vereen's class have reading problems, but Pooch has it the worst. "Oh Lord," said Libby, "we're gonna be here all day waiting for Pooch to get through the first sentence."

"Shut up, you all," Hattie told Libby and the folks around us. "Pooch," she whispered loudly, "that man's the one Big Head is gonna be in the church play Friday night, remember? Big Head can tell you what the man did if you want to be him. Go ahead and try."

"Well, lemme see that paper. Do I gotta wear my hair like his, too?" Pooch strutted up to Miz Thomas, took the speech from her, and started back for his seat.

"Wait, you don't have the part yet, man," Jamal told him. "You got to read what's on that sheet."

"I was . . . I was . . . what's that word, Miz Thomas?" said Pooch.

"Born," she said. "And children, the boy in the church play has a name. It's Jeff, not Big Head, thank you." Everybody laughed and looked at Hattie. Big Head is Miz Thomas's son.

"I was born in—what's this one?"

"Let somebody else read," said Jamal.

"I can do it." Pooch twisted the paper around. "The light's just not right in here, that's all."

"Well, you tried." Miz Thomas smiled at him. "What about you, Jamal?"

Jamal shook his head. Joey Hollenstein raised his hand. "Can I try?"

"Oh, not you, Joey," said Miz Vereen. "We need—uh—a—"

"Of course, you can," said Miz Thomas. She

handed him the sheet, and he read it quickly. He is a good reader anyway, from Miz Cutterhorn's class. But I frowned. Why would Joey want to play Frederick Douglass? Joey is Jewish, like Ernie. Miz Vereen said they were, lots of times. See, whenever she talked about Jewish people and something about some war, she'd say, "And let's remember Joey and Ernie, our fine Jewish boys, and what their people have gone through, bless their hearts."

Joey would just sit there, and Ernie's face would turn red.

Miz Vereen and Miz Thomas got to whispering and nodding and shaking their heads. "But I look at it like this, Miz Vereen," said Miz Thomas. "If a child wants a part, that child'll have a chance for it if he or she is here. Don't you think so?"

"No, I don't," said Miz Vereen, frowning a little.

Miz Thomas waved at Miz Stokes to come over, and the three of them whispered and nodded and shook their heads. Then Miz Stokes patted Miz Vereen on the shoulder and walked away. Miz Vereen stopped frowning. She smiled and nodded at Miz Thomas. "I understand now," she said.

"Who else wants to try for Frederick Douglass?" Miz Thomas asked. "No one? Joey, it's yours."

Next was the role of Harriet Tubman. Harriet Tubman had something to do with slavery, I knew.

Whoever played her would probably have to wear old clothes, have a rag around her head, be bare-foot, or wear beat-up runover boots. My second cousin Yolanda Fence McCray, who palled around with Kenyatta, tried first. I was surprised that *she'd* want to look like that! She always dresses so fancy. Her granddaddy is a city councilman. One time she came to school upset because her momma made her wear stockings that Yolanda said had a big hole in the left leg. That hole was so tiny you had to put your eye right up against her leg to see it.

While Yolanda read, I talked to Alicia about what was for lunch. Yolanda walked back with a big smile on her face when Miz Thomas said she got the part. Kenyatta got the part of a woman named True something. She sat down smiling left and right. They acted like getting those parts was a big deal. I wondered why.

Jermaine Walker got the part of Dr. King. I wasn't surprised. His big brother Dexter got the part in the church program. Jermaine and Dexter are our pastor Rev. Walker's kids.

Alicia Valendez got the part of somebody named Marian Anderson. "Did you really want her?" I whispered when she came back. "Won't you feel funny?"

"Funny how? 'Cause I'm gonna play a Black lady? So? Joey Hollenstein's playing that Douglass guy, and Joey's Jewish. Larry Washington's playing Ben Franklin and Larry's Black."

"Yeah, but you and Joey's not anybody important."

"Are you crazy? What do you mean?" She puffed up. "I am, too! Miz Thomas said Marian Anderson was an internationally known singer. Didn't you hear?"

"Sure," I said, though I hadn't. I decided to sit up a little straighter and listen a little harder.

Miz T and Miz Riley came over to listen to our group. They'd been doing that all over the cafeteria. Miz Vereen was talking now. "And now we need a few of my precious little Black friends to be in a special skit."

"What special skit?" said Miz Thomas. She leaned over to look at a paper in Miz Vereen's hand.

"You'll have sacks and be slaves," said Miz Vereen. "And as you walk in one by one into the rice fields, you'll sing 'Swing Low, Sweet Chariot.' Then you'll go to another field, pick cotton, and sing 'Dixie.' "

"I ain't gonna be no slave!" Jamal frowned up, folded his arms across his chest, and kicked out his feet.

"I'm not picking cotton in *nobody's* play!" said Timika.

Well, there Miz Vereen went again, I thought, and felt sick. Talking about slaves again. I prayed she wouldn't call my name.

"Yes, I think this can fit in nicely with our southern heritage," Miz Vereen told us, smiling. "I wrote this skit myself, and we performed it at the other school. See, right at this spot they could sing 'Dixie,' and some of them could march in with our Confederate flag—"

Miz Thomas shook her head. "No, I don't think so. I'm sorry."

"Why not?" Miz Vereen said.

Miss T came over to Miz Vereen and whispered something to her. "Oh!" Miz Vereen's cheeks got as red as Cupid's wings. She clapped her hands to her face. "Oh, of course, I'm so sorry. Oh, children, I'm sorry. I just thought that . . . never mind."

Miz T and Miz Thomas patted Miz Vereen's shoulder. People did that a lot to her.

"Now! Who's for being Dr. Mary McLeod Bethune?" asked Miz Thomas. "She was the first woman in the whole country to establish a college."

Timika tried for that one, but lost out to somebody from Miz Thomas's class. "Next is Alexander Morgan G. 'Gumbo' Dickson' our town's—"

"Me! Me! Oh, please, me!" Pooch jumped up and tore toward Miz Thomas. "You just gotta give

✳ 45 ✳

Gumbo Dickson to me. My sister Bunny kinda helped to find him, remember?"

Miz Vereen and Miz Thomas got together and whispered again. "Well, Pooch, if you're that determined, then you're the one to do it," said Miz Vereen. "You *are* Gumbo Dickson! Though how you'll learn your part I'll never know."

CHAPTER

FOUR

I wished Miz Thomas and Miz Vereen would get the Black History section finished so we could try out for narrators. I raised my hand and asked to get a drink of water.

"All right, but hurry," Miz Vereen said.

I took my time getting to the water fountain. It was at the other side of the cafeteria. I passed Hattie and the other kids in the rappers corner, rapping, "We're here to say/That on this day/A mighty man was born."

Draped nearby around Miz Riley at the piano was the special chorus, talking out words to a song. When I went past the Washington and Lincoln characters group, I heard Brandy say, "I bet it starts like this. Like, 'I am the wife of the first president of the United States. I'm Martha Washington.' And then she probably says something about what she uses to wax her floors."

Everybody around her laughed. I wished I could be in her group.

I was glad Miz Thomas hadn't let that cotton picker stuff stay in. Sometimes Miz Thomas can be okay.

My Black third-grade teacher Miz Smith didn't hang up a single poster of Dr. King last year, not even on his birthday. She didn't hang any posters of anybody during Black History Month or even mention it last year. I don't think she much liked posters or pictures of anybody or anything, though. She just kept pictures of George Washington, Abraham Lincoln, and a little picture of Ronald Reagan and George Bush on the wall, and that was it. Not even a poster of a dinosaur or a dog—just numbers and letters. She was still nice.

Miz Thomas and Miz Nisby were always talking about Black this and Black that. Miz Nisby kept posters of Bill Cosby and Dr. King up in the library all year long. She had movies and film strips with US in them all school year, not just in February during Black History Month. February is when almost everybody in school and at church and on TV pulled out stuff about Black History. Black, Black,

Black everywhere! And then we don't hear hardly anything anymore about it until the next February.

That stuff is okay with me if it's about us doing what everybody else does. Miz Vereen shows a lot of movies, too. But sometimes Miz Vereen shows pictures of real poor Black folks with great big teeth sitting on old broken down front porches with their hair messy, eating watermelon and grinning, juice running down their arms, garbage all around the yard. Or she shows us those old history movies about South Carolina, and Black folks in them are slaves or always sweeping floors, dancing in great big shoes, or wearing rags around their heads.

I also hate having to read books or stories that show dead Black people hanging from tree limbs, or German shepherd dogs biting on them. It seems like she shows movies and books like that more than any other teacher I've had.

And another thing, said Mary Inside. It's really yucky when Miz Vereen has filmstrips about starving Africans and Indians, because they're always shown with flies crawling on their faces, white crud around their mouths, and big bellies. Nasty!

Kids would laugh, or point and say, "There you go, Jamal," or "That woman looks just like your momma!" Pooch and them would call each other "fly-faced African." I want to crawl under my desk when stuff like that comes around. It's awfully embarrassing to me. I wonder if the other kids in class think those starving people are kin to us. No sir, they sure aren't, not to me!

It makes me think there's something wrong with those Black people in those books and on TV to make them get such a lowdown deal, you know? And then I get scared. Does that mean there is something wrong with me? Will bad things happen to me, too?

Shoot, I want to be like Brandy and Buffy and Ashley and them. I hardly ever see pictures of their people getting beat up or getting hung, or being real, real poor, except on the "Beverly Hillbillies," and even then they were rich.

I got my drink of water and walked back slowly until I saw Alicia waving at me. I hurried up.

"And now we need to take care of that last narrator," Miz Vereen was saying when I got to my seat. "Oh, there you are, Mary Elouise. We were looking for you. I'm going to ask you to be our narrator."

What? I got a narrator part and I hadn't read a word! Boy, did I have some pull with Miz Vereen. I was gonna really thank Hattie. I bet she said something to Miz Vereen, and Miz Vereen said something to Miz Thomas. I stumbled up to Miz Vereen and reached for the sheets of paper in her hand.

"Yes, dear. We knew you'd do an excellent job with this particular narrator part, so we saved it just for you," she said. "You're our narrator for the Black History segment."

My eyebrows flew up and my mouth popped open. I shook my head and rubbed my eyes in disbelief.

"What's the matter, dear?" Miz Vereen asked. "Something in your eye?"

"I . . . I don't want *this* one."

"What's the matter with *this* one?" said Miz Thomas. "It's a very good part."

I stared at the floor. "I wanted to narrate the Love Month part or the Presidents part."

"Kimiko Johnson got the Love Month, and George Dozier got the Presidents," Miz Thomas said. "I believe you left just when we started with narrators. It wouldn't have been fair to have made everybody wait till you got back. You've got a real good part, honey. Hattie said you'd like it."

I just shook my head.

Miz Thomas took the papers. "Okay. So, children, Mary Elouise doesn't want this part. Anybody who does?"

"I do!" Libby snake-hipped up to Miz Thomas. "Let me, please, please." Miz Thomas told her to read just the first page. She took the papers and began to read, but got the giggles and had to stop. "Thank you, Libby," Miz Thomas said. "Anybody else? No?"

I glanced at Miz Vereen, who smiled and nodded at me. "Go ahead, dear," she said. I sighed hard, inside.

I took the papers from Libby and tried to rush through the words. They were hard, though, so I made a lot of mistakes. I looked back at Miz Vereen. She smiled and nodded again.

"Between Libby lisping it through her braces and Mary Elouise galloping through it, I don't know how we can decide which one ought to get it," I heard Miz Thomas whisper to Miz Vereen.

"Let me try again," Libby begged. She went through the first page without laughing this time.

"Much better." Miz Thomas cocked her head at me. "Care to try it again?"

I looked down at the sheet. Oh no! I said to myself. Slave. I hadn't seen that word the time before. I looked at Miz Thomas.

I looked over at Miz Vereen again, dying to beg her to give me one of the other narrator parts.

"Mary Elouise, come on, sugar dumpling," she said.

"Come on, sugar dumpling," I heard Pepper repeat, and giggle.

"Or do you want to give in and let Libby have it?" Miz Thomas said.

I slid my eyes over at Libby. Give in to Libby? And give away my chance with Brandy?

I lifted my shoulders, took a deep breath and

read again. I think I made as many mistakes this time as I did the last time, though.

"Miz Thomas, what do you think?" Miz Vereen said.

"I think we can find something for you somewhere else in our Presidents Month play, Libby," Miz Thomas said. "Thank you. Mary Elouise, congratulations. You're our Black History narrator."

I clumped back to my seat, happy and mad at the same time. I rolled my eyes at Alicia. "I didn't want *that* one!"

"That's what Hattie said you've been talking about," she replied. "Got to be a narrator, got to be a narrator! I bet you didn't tell her which one. I heard her beg and beg Miz Vereen to get you a narrator part, and now you don't want it."

"If you hate the part that much, maybe you can swap with Kimiko or George," Lonnie Lee said. "I'll go tell her you're coming over." She slid over to the table behind and to the right of us where Kimiko sat.

When Miz Vereen and Miz Thomas went into another conference, I slipped over to her and Kimiko. "I, unh, wondered if you might wanna swap parts," I said to Kimiko.

"Naw," Kimiko said. "Anyway, we can't change around unless Miz Vereen or Miz Thomas say so. You don't want your part?"

"No, she doesn't, 'cause it's about Black History," said Lonnie Lee, "and she gets embarrassed even when the word Black comes up. She about goes through the floor."

"I do not!" My face burned. "It's 'cause I—my part's five pages long."

"Mine's almost seven. Do your own part, Mary Elouise. It's about you guys, anyway."

Miz Vereen saw us. "My dears, what are you doing over there? Come back to your seats, please."

Just then the kids in the other groups came back, rapping and singing. Everything got real loud. I slipped in with them and saw Brandy. "I got a narrator part," I told her when she went past.

"I'm wigged out," she said.

I followed behind her, trying to keep up. "Well, see ya in class." I hurried on to my seat. "Brandy said she was wigged out over my part," I told Alicia when I got back. "How about that?"

"Whoop de do," said Alicia. "What did Kimiko say? No? Then try George."

"But Miz Vereen said I gotta stay here!"

"Send him a note."

I tore a piece of paper out of my notebook and carefully printed, "George, let's us swap narrator parts, OK? Mary Elouise, 4C."

After folding the note seven times, I wrote *George Dozier* on one side and gave it to Lonnie

Lee, who passed it to Chaundra, who passed it on to Pepper, who dropped it on the floor! Bubba put his fat foot on it, picked it up, and started to read it.

"Pass it on, Bubba," Alicia hissed.

Just as the note reached George's fingers at the next cluster of tables across from me, Miz Thomas said sharply, "George, please bring me what you have in your hands."

George jumped right up and handed her the note, along with his glasses, and a Transformers eraser that he also had in his hands. Miz Thomas read the note, then looked me hard in the eye. Our section got real quiet. Boy, was I in trouble now. I hunched down and waited.

"Mary Elouise, if you don't want the part, give it up right now. I certainly don't want you to *have* to do it."

"Well." I took a deep breath, remembering Brandy. "Yes m'am," I said real low, "I want the part."

"What?" Suddenly Miz Thomas got deaf, and I had to repeat what I said.

Miz Cutterhorn told us to be sure to tell our parents the play would be at 3:00 P.M. Friday, February 5. Notes would go home in a few days, too, and didn't the play sound exciting?

Yeah, yeah.

When rehearsal was over, Miz Vereen told us to walk back to our room like little ladies and gentlemen, but I let my feet go just any which way. When we came into the front lobby, I looked at our gigantic hand tree painted on the wall. My green hand print was still there. Back in first grade, we dipped our hands in green and brown paint, then smushed them against the wall in the shape of a ten-foot tree. Our green hands were leaves and our brown hands were the trunk and branches. Across the top of the tree our art teacher Miz Haney had written in red paint, "Reaching Greater Heights."

I sure didn't feel like I could reach any heights that day.

I banged myself against the hand tree a couple times. "Don't be so upset," Alicia said. "You could have ended up a bone or a ball of string. Now, *that* would be embarrassing!"

"Yeah, I guess you're right. Maybe."

But I wanted to tell her that there were also embarrassing words I'd have to say, the kind of words Miz Vereen liked to use, like "lowly beginnings." But I just kept it to myself. Alicia wouldn't understand. I couldn't wait to talk to Hattie about her getting me the wrong part.

But as soon as we got out of the school building, Hattie turned to me and started bawling me out! Boy, was she burned up! "Mary Elouise, I won't ever give a teacher your name for anything anymore. I heard what happened. That you were hunching and jumping up there like you do in class and acting so ignorant." She waved at Maizell to hurry over to us. "That slave stuff happened a way long time ago. You get too upset about that stuff. See, it doesn't bother me. You ought to be around Raisin more."

Hattie's older sister Raisin and ole Miz Effie Pfluggins, who lives up the road, like to walk around in cemeteries and talk about who was buried there.

"Hunh!" I shook my head hard. "And next thing, she'd be trying to get me in that old cemetery."

Hattie laughed. "Some stuff she does is interesting, though. Like she found out where our great-great-great grandparents were buried. They're buried over in a cemetery outside Conway. At Christmas, Grandma Stackhouse came over and told us about them. She said they'd been slaves."

Poor Hattie. "Don't you feel weird, knowing that?"

"Weird about what?" Hattie frowned hard at me. "Nothing's weird about that. Big deal. So were yours!"

I wanted to say she was wrong, but I didn't know. So I kept quiet.

We all were quiet for a few minutes, just slapping our feet against the sidewalk and the dirt. Finally Maizell said, "Is Miz Vereen mean?"

Hattie unpuffed herself a little to answer. "No,

she's mostly nice. Mary Elouise is her little teacher's pet."

"Am not!"

"I'm just joking, girl. Hey, I know what you mean about getting upset when folks start stuff about slavery and then eyeball *you*." Hattie turned to Maizell. "Miz Vereen says some awful crazy stuff."

"Yeah," I added, "like sugar dumplings and sugar plums and stuff, too."

"If *you* get Miz Vereen next year, Maizell, don't you pay attention to her crazy talk, hear? And Mary Elouise, just don't pay Miz Vereen any attention when she talks funny, okay? I don't. Not too much. Nothing you can do about it anyway. She's the teacher."

But then I got worried about something else just as bad.

"I still wish I could have got one of those other narrator parts."

Hattie slapped her hand against her forehead. "Here we go again."

"Hattie, please!"

I must have looked so pitiful that she felt sorry for me. She snapped her fingers. "You got any money?"

"Only seventy-five cents, from my Christmas money."

"Maybe if you gave it to Kimiko or George they'd switch parts with you."

"I can't do that. That's bribery."

"Okay." Hattie turned up her nose. "Do it your way."

I followed behind for a few steps, thinking, then I caught up. "Do you think it'd work?"

"Trust me." Hattie grinned. "Now here's what you tell them when you give the money to them. Do Kimiko first."

"Okay." We came to my house. "See you tomorrow, and hey, thanks, okay?"

"What would you do without me, girl?" Hattie said back. She and Maizell ran up the street.

At recess Friday morning, I ran over to where Kimiko was playing dodgeball. "Can I talk to you for a minute?" I said, trying to whisper real low.

"What?" Kimiko wrinkled up her nose. "What?"

I sighed hard. "I'll give you this if you swap parts with me." I dropped three quarters in her hand, and rolled her fingers up around them quick so nobody could see me do it.

Kimiko opened her hand and squinted at the money. "But—"

"Look, you just took it, so we just swapped, see? Now you tell Miz Vereen you don't want your part and you want me to have it. Okay, Kimiko? Please?"

"I don't think—"

The bell rang just then, ending recess. I hurried away, and we lined up at the door. I smiled at

Kimiko, and gave her the thumbs-up sign. We hurried back inside to the rest rooms, and then to our rooms. I had barely got back into our room good when Miz Vereen called me up to her desk.

"Kimiko just popped in and told me you gave her some money to switch parts," she said. "Shame on you!"

Shocked and embarrassed, I slunk to my seat. Bubba rubbed his forefingers across each other. "Shame on you!" he said in a high-pitched voice.

I could have choked him. Could have choked Kimiko, too. I didn't even get my money back.

Then Miz Vereen told us it was Dr. King's birthday. She said a few words about him, then got off into talking about what life was like in the old days. She didn't say anything embarrassing, though, and that was a relief.

When sixth-period art class came around, my name was called over the intercom to come to the office. I was glad to go. That meant Momma had come to take me to spend the weekend with my grandmother, Big Momma. She lives on Cuffy's Island. Momma picks me up early from school, while it was still light, in the winter. She doesn't like to be out on the ferry at night. I didn't mind leaving art. I wasn't real good at it.

I've spent weekends with Big Momma as far back as I can remember. I'm her favorite grandkid.

Big Momma is my father Big Mike Avery's mother. Big Momma has arthritis in her hands, and sugar diabetes. I help her around the house, too, when we aren't fishing or crabbing in her creek. She was born in North Carolina, up around Beaufort. Granddaddy Avery, who is dead, was a fisherman. He used to have his own fishing boat and went up and down the coast from the Outer Banks and Cape Hatteras to Florida, she said. I never met him.

Maybe Big Momma can help me straighten out this mess I was in over this Black History. Maybe she can even give me some tips about how to be best friends with Brandy.

I gathered up my books and bag, got my coat, said good-bye to Miz Vereen and Hattie, and headed for the office. There was Momma, all right, talking with Miz Thomas.

"Come in, come in, Miz Avery," Miz Thomas said to Momma. "Can you stay for a minute to chat? Happy Martin Luther King Day! You come in, too, Mary Elouise."

But I was afraid of that look in Miz Thomas's eye. What was she going to tell Momma? "Momma, don't we need to get on out to Big Momma's?"

"I'm not in any great hurry," Momma said. We followed Miz Thomas into Miz T's office. "I sure do like this school," Momma said, calling Miz

Thomas Johnnie Mae, her first name. Miz Thomas thanked her and called her by her first name, too.

"Now." Miz Thomas looked at me. "Mary Elouise, Kimiko said to give this to you." She handed me the three quarters. I froze. I bet they were even the same coins, with my fingerprints all over them. When I wouldn't take the money, she piled them in a little stack on her desk in front of me.

Miz Thomas told Momma about the play and me trying to change parts by bribing Kimiko. I slouched lower and lower in the chair until I nearly sat on my back.

"I can't imagine you acting like this," Momma told me. "Johnnie Mae, you know how mousy-like Mary Elouise is. She wouldn't have the nerve to bribe anybody." She looked at me sharp. "Where'd you get money to bribe anybody? You told me you'd spent up all your Christmas money."

"I did, Momma! Well, all the dollar bill parts."

"What dollar bill—"

Miz Thomas broke in. "Maybe Mary Elouise can explain why she wants to change parts. Why don't you tell us?"

You can believe that I did not say a word.

Neither did Momma.

Miz Thomas waited, then she softly cleared her throat. "Shenetta, Mary Elouise is embarrassed about her Black History narrator's part in our Presidents Month play. In that section, we highlight the achievements of Black Americans like Dr. King—"

"Who was the light in the midst of the darkness for us," Momma smiled. Then she stopped and frowned. "Wait a minute. Mary Elouise, what play? Embarrassed about what?"

I wished I could roll down to the floor, slide under the door and be gone quick from there! But Momma and Miz Thomas had nailed me to the chair with their eyes.

"Johnnie Mae, tell me about the play," said Momma, still frowning.

Miz Thomas told her. Then she said, "Well, Shenetta, how shall I tell you *this*?"

"Real quick." Momma crimped her lips down at the ends and crossed her arms.

"Well, I think Mary Elouise has a LIT-tle attitude problem, but it can be worked out. I've seen many children be like this."

Momma looked surprised. "Be like what?"

"Oh, be ashamed about one thing or the other. Kids think they're too tall, too short, too fat, too skinny, too poor, too dark-skinned, too light-skinned—too something! You know, how they feel about themselves. Sometimes we adults act like we're ashamed of them, or say negative things to them without meaning to, see what I'm saying? Happens all the time. But parents and teachers are human." She leaned forward. "And we certainly have no need of being ashamed of who we are, do we, Shenetta?"

Momma stared at Miz Thomas. "Is what you're saying part of this play?"

Miz Thomas shook her head slowly. She drummed her fingers on her desk, then picked up a pencil and began writing on a sheet of paper on her desk. "Shenetta, what color of doll does Mary Elouise play with? White or Black?"

"M'am?" said Momma.

"What color—"

"Johnnie Mae Thomas, she plays with whatever we can afford to buy, that's what color. Look here," she said, standing up and pulling her coat together, "Mary Elouise doesn't have any LIT-tle attitude problem. I don't understand how you're trying to mix together all this stuff because she gave a girl some money."

Momma marched to the door. "Well, people." That was her favorite expression when she was really mad. "You got some nerve, Johnnie Mae Thomas! If you think Mary Elouise is ashamed of her race, you don't row with both oars in the water!"

Momma shot out of the room and down the hallway. Her thick-soled work shoes thumped on the floor, and her green uniform skirt shook every time she took a step. She was that mad.

I followed, embarrassed and pleased at the same time. Momma sure told Miz Thomas off, even if she was wrong.

We got into our car. "That woman is a trip!" Momma slammed her foot to the gas pedal. We leaped away from the curb in a cloud of blue smoke. "She's off her rocker!" We screeched around a corner. "Who does she think she is, talking about you being ashamed of your race, and what kind of doll do you play with?"

I hoped she wouldn't ask me to answer that question. I hoped she'd just take me straight out to Big Momma's. And Lord knows I hoped she wouldn't start talking about that seventy-five cents. Momma watches every penny that comes in and goes out of the house like a hawk on a mouse. Bribing kids was not on her list of ways to spend money.

"By the way, where is that little ole doll Big Momma gave you for Christmas?"

My breath got tight in my throat. "What doll?"

"You know, that little ole Black Cabbage Patch doll Big Momma bought you last time, the one so ugly in the face it was pretty."

"Oh, that one. I, unh, well, I don't know."

"You don't know? Christmas was just last month. Where is that doll?"

"Unh, it, I, well, it got wet in the yard."

The car jumped when her foot hit the gas again. "Got wet in the yard how?"

"It got left out there."

"Your grandmomma spent good money on that doll. When she buys you Black dolls something always happens to them. The one she bought for you before somehow got dropped behind the car and I ran over the poor thing's head. The one before that got dropped in the creek. Nothing like that happens to the white ones. How did this last Black one get left in the yard and when?"

"Unh, I don't remember."

"I'm not gonna stand for any more foolishness today, Mary Elouise Avery. Tell me the truth."

I took a deep breath. "It got left day after Christmas 'cause I forgot and left it on the porch and the wind or something must have knocked it off in the yard and it started to rain and it rained for three days, and that's how it got wet." Take my soul to Jesus, because my behind was Momma's now, for sure!

"Why didn't you tell me? We could have dried it out somehow. What did you do with it?"

"Put it in the dumpster over by the Gumbo Limbo Soda Fountain and Cafe."

"You what? My goodness' sakes, you sure got an ill temper against Black dolls, don't you." She cut her eyes at me. "And tell me why."

If I told her I didn't like Black dolls period, she'd get madder than a hornet, I bet. So I said, " 'Cause this one was too ugly."

"Well, people. Everybody already knew the doll was ugly. You could see that on TV. That's why people bought them—because they were ugly. That *ugly* doll you begged and begged for cost Big Momma forty or fifty some dollars. You didn't have enough gumption to admit you didn't want the Black one. No, you let her buy it, and then you left it in the yard 'cause it was too ugly."

Momma's face looked so evil she looked like Ole Green Alice, the Halloween witch I read about last year. "Nobody leaves you out in the yard 'cause you're too ugly, do they? I swear, you're such a stupid little ole ugly Black thing. You don't have any more sense than that doll."

Momma carried on like that, calling me names and talking mean, until I huddled up against the car door and started to cry. Then she stopped. We rode along not saying anything. I felt like a piece of dirt, not worth a penny.

Finally she said something. "Mary Elouise, honey, I didn't mean to call you names. It's just that Big Momma doesn't have money like that to throw away. I didn't mean to talk so nasty. I'm sorry." She looked real sad. "I'm sorry, okay? You're not stupid or ugly or anything. Ain't nothin' wrong being dark-skinned, either."

I didn't say anything. When kids called each other stupid or ugly or Black, it was one thing. When your own mother called you names like that, it was worse, like it was true. She made me feel ashamed that I had this ole dark skin. I wished I was light-skinned, like she was, or white.

She put her hand on my arm. "Mary Elouise, I'm sorry. But that's why Miz Thomas was asking about the color of your dolls and talking about not being ashamed. She was right, too. Ashamed! I bet you are, though I'm sure Lord don't know why. Now I feel like a fool all over again, with this going on right under my nose."

I just kept my mouth shut. There wasn't anything I could say to change anything now.

We shot up Fifteenth Street toward home. "Well, we have got to do something about it," she said.

I wanted to ask what this "something" was that she planned to work on, but I kept quiet. I figured I was going to be involved somehow, no matter which way she went.

"And we're gonna start with your part in this play."

See? I sat up straight. Could she make them give me another part? That'd be great. Or make them take me out of the play? That'd be awful.

"We're gonna take that Black History narrator part—"

I glanced over at Momma, hoping.

"And you're gonna get up on that stage and do it so everybody'll know that you're not ashamed," she said.

My face crumpled up. We pulled up to our house. I was so mad I could have chewed nails. Thank you, Dr. Martin Luther King, Jr.! said Mary Inside. Look what your birthday got me into!

CHAPTER

FIVE

Why did things always have to get complicated when I wanted something simple? All I wanted to be was Brandy's best friend. But here I was now with a part I didn't want, Momma calling me names and mad at me about those dolls, Miz Vereen believing I was bribing, and Miz Thomas saying I had a LIT-tle attitude problem.

"Momma, would you please, please not tell Big Momma about the dolls? I—I didn't mean to throw them away. I just—I just—well, I just don't like that kind."

"Big Momma thought this last doll was truly what you wanted." Momma sounded sad. "She took money out of her Social Security check to buy it for you. No, I'm not going to breathe a word of it to her. It would hurt her so. And don't you, either. You ought to be ashamed to not like dolls of your own color. They're just like you."

Mary Inside said, I don't want to play with anything that's just like me. You just said I was a stupid ugly ole Black thing, remember?

Momma told me to get our house key out of her purse so she could carry the sack of groceries. We left the car and walked up on the porch. I went all through her purse, looking for the key. No key.

"The key, Mary Elouise, the key. And the telephone's ringing." She sniffed at the door. "Smells like somebody left the coffee maker on and it's dry! Did you guys use the coffee maker to fix hot chocolate again? Come on, girl, open the door. I got to use the bathroom, too." She hopped from one foot to the other.

I searched through my own pockets for my key. No key there, either. I bet Argentina had it again.

"Please open the door before I wet up the porch." Momma set the sack down.

"Momma, your key ain't in here!"

Momma grabbed the purse and scraped around in it. Then she jumped around to the kitchen window to see if it was open. We'd gone through the window before when we'd got locked out. Wouldn't you know, the windows were locked this time. So was the back door.

"Maybe we should wait for Argentina," I said. She should have some kind of key."

"But I'm sure there's something in there burning, and you know Argentina might be half the night coming home." We waited for a few minutes. I looked up and down the street. No Argentina. I didn't see the boys either, but they don't have a key, so they couldn't have helped.

"Well, people." Momma hurried to the car, pulled the crowbar from under the seat where she kept it when she had to be out at night. She forced the thin, sharp end of the crowbar into the crack between the door and the wall. She pushed hard against the crowbar handle four or five times. Nothing. Taking a deep breath, she tried again.

Blam! Wood splinters flew everywhere when the door popped open. Momma ran to the kitchen and unplugged the coffee maker. She zipped into the bathroom shouting, "Get the phone!"

And wouldn't you know the phone stopped before I could get to it?

I wrote the date of the play on the calendar in the hallway. Everybody had New Africa Number 1 Missionary Baptist Church calendars like this one. On the cover was a color picture of our church and Choir Number Three. It listed brthdays and wedding dates of practically all the Black folks in the county, even the ones who weren't Baptists. My birthdate is March 12. It says so right in the little box beneath the number. Nobody else has a birthday or a wedding listed on that day but me. It also lists dates about Black History, but I never read much of that stuff. Hattie's birthday is April 16, and Pooch's is December 16. I don't know when Brandy's is. Her name isn't on the calendar, anyway.

"Pack that yellow jumper, your good shoes, and that white long-sleeved blouse with the mice on the collar," said Momma, "so we can get on out to Big Momma's."

"Oh, I get that jumper! All right! I can wear it to church on Sunday."

"To church tonight, too, Mary Elouise. Did you forget about the Dr. King Memorial tonight at church? It starts at seven o'clock. You can change when we go pick up Big Momma, then we can swing on back to this side for church."

Shoot. I'd planned to watch wrestling on Channel 66 at Big Momma's. She loves wrestling, too. Big Momma has a color TV so big it looks like it was built up out of the floor. She has a fluffy, light blue shag rug with lots of pillows, right in front of the TV. You know where I spend my time.

But I was kind of curious to see how everybody would do in the program. I wasn't in it, of course. I didn't want to be. But the boys and Argentina were, which was why Momma was in such a fiddle.

"Argentina was supposed to have been to Miz Erma's Kut and Kurl by noon to get her hair done, and be here by two o'clock to get her clothes ready," Momma said. "It's after three now." She poked her head in our closet. "Hasn't been back to do a thing for herself."

I knew the boys were at Johnson Barbershop getting their hair cut. They loved to go, too. They'd come back with zigzags and letters cut in their flattop haircuts.

In the kitchen I found a note with red, blue, and green hearts taped to the refrigerator. "She's been here," I hollered. "She left you a note." I gave it to Momma.

"Dear Momma," the note read. "After I get through at the Ebonettes I'm going over to Bunny's house. If I'm not there, I'm at Big Boy's. Be back in a minute."

Momma looked at the clock on the stove. "Ebonettes? That's where they do those wild hairdos. She was supposed to have gone to Miz Erma's. Argentina," she said to the note, "you should've been back ages ago."

She called over to Bunny's house, then over to Big Boy's. "You be home in five minutes, Argentina," she said into the telephone. "A promise is a promise. Argentina, don't play with me, and no, don't blow me *no* kisses. You come home now!"

I stuffed what else I wanted to take with me to

Big Momma's in two big grocery sacks. Then I folded up my blouse, slip, and my new jumper, and stuck them in another one.

Oh, I'd almost forgot my mouse pin I'd begged Momma to get me for Christmas. She did, too, but that was all she bought. The rest was stuff she said I needed, like clothes and junk. Depending on which way you looked at the pin, the mouse's glass eyes flashed red, gold, green, and blue sparkles. Gold animal jewelry pins were the thing at school. Brandy had a mouse pin, too. Kenyatta and Yolanda had dog pins. Hattie didn't have one. She said they cost too much.

Antoine and Andrew rolled into the yard on their scooters, fussing over who was the best rapper.

"Got to be Public Enemy, man!"

"No, man, they're old. Got to be Ruff'n Tuffer!"

Then they started to beebop, loud, and slap their legs in time to the words.

They blasted in through the back door into the kitchen. I went in to see how they looked. "Whoa, you know better," Momma said to them. "Hold down on that noise. Your hair looks nice. I like how the barbers do those little rat tails in the back, boys. Turn around and let me see the front."

Antoine grinned. "Momma, Public Enemy's got a new song out, and it's baaad!" He and Andrew spun around and started into the song, be-bopping, but Momma stopped them.

"I'm gonna public enemy you if you don't polish your white shoes and get ready for the program. Mary Elouise, you run their bath water. I gotta get their shirts ironed. Argentina was supposed to iron them last night."

Just as I was about to go into the bathroom, Momma turned to me. "How come I'm just now hearing about you being in this play at school? And what's this woman talking about, you not liking Dr. King and so on?"

"I like Dr. King," I said. Oh boy, here we go again. I just stood there with my head down and felt sick.

"Hey, what happened to our door?" Argentina waltzed into the kitchen. "Mommie, am I late? I called and called and called but nobody answered the phone." She danced over to Momma and kissed her on the cheek. "How do you all like my 'do? Mary Elouise, I borrowed your key. Here." She dropped it in my hand, shot into our room, and closed the door.

Zoom in. Zoom out. That was Argentina, all right. Momma and I were both speechless over her hair. Most of her long, thick hair was swooped over to the left side of her head, and pinned with a fancy red comb. The ends hung down in tight, shiny curls over her left eye. The hair at the back of her neck was twisted into a long braid and snaked down in front of her chest.

She looked so sharp. I wished hard that I could get my hair to be pretty like that.

"Argentina, who said you could go to Ebonettes? Not me!" Momma said through the door. "What did you tell them to do to your hair? You can't wear your hair like that to church. You look like you're ready to go to some party. Argentina, open this door!"

She rattled the doorknob until Argentina opened it. Momma went in, and I followed, ready to hear the bawling out Argentina was going to get.

As Momma fussed, Argentina just sat and nodded her head, and smiled. Finally Momma said, "Well, I guess it's been done now."

She touched the braid. "Guess it doesn't look all that wild. Girl, you're something else." Momma spied me. "We got to get moving. Mary Elouise, did you run the boys' water?"

In the bathroom, I swished my fingers in the water, wishing Momma would let me go to Ebonettes to get my hair done. She only let me go to Miz Erma's to turn the ends under for Christmas, Easter, and funerals. Miz Erma was so old-fashioned! She only did little ole ladies' hair—and mine. Hattie didn't even go to her anymore. Momma said doing my hair was a waste of time and good money because I sweated it back up too much. She did it herself the rest of the time.

I sighed. Maybe one of these days I'd be able to grow lots and lots of hair like Argentina, or Libby, or Brandy, and wear it scooped up on top of my head.

"You—Andrew and Antoine—come get in this tub!"

Between Argentina and Momma fussing over which dress Argentina would wear, and me trying to help dress the boys, we were nearly an hour late leaving the house. Then we had to wait until the drawbridge came down so we could drive on it to Turner's Isle. We missed Mr. Montegue's ferry going out, so we had to wait for it to return to take us over to Cuffy's Island.

When we finally rolled into Big Momma's driveway, I saw her outside on the porch under the porch light, sitting in her rocking chair. Bullet, her Great Dane, sat right beside her. Big Momma's big black fur coat was wrapped tight around her, and she wore her black fuzzy dress hat. She had on her burgundy high heels, too, and matching purse. Big Momma loved to dress sharp. She was tapping her high heel. We all waved.

"Big Momma, what're you doing out here in the cold?" Momma hollered out the car window. "It's still January, you know. Get in quick."

"Don't rush me, Shenetta Avery. You're the one late," Big Momma said. She stood up, stepped carefully down the stairs and took short steps to the car. She called that her high heel walk. She carried her dress cane on one arm and her purse on the other.

"Hey, Namesake, how you makin' it?" she said to me. "Give me some sugar." She leaned down to the window.

"Hey, Big Momma." I leaned my head out and gave Big Momma a kiss on the cheek.

Big Mike, our dad, had named me Mary Elouise after her. He was killed in a car wreck right after Antoine and Andrew were born. I was two years old. Big Momma talked about him a lot, and so did Momma. They said he was a good dad, and that we kids should never forget him. Big Momma said I looked just like him. He was her son. She said I looked like her, too. She was dark-skinned, too. That made me feel good.

"Mary Elouise, just leave your clothes in the car," said Momma. "You don't need to change, since you're not in the program and we're running so late. C'mon, get in, Big Momma. Argentina, get out and help her in."

Argentina and I looked down at my skirt. There were spaghetti sauce drops on it from lunch, and chalk dust from the eraser fight I'd had with Pooch.

When Argentina told Momma my skirt was dirty, Momma said that I should keep my coat on. "Nobody'll see it, honey. C'mon, we're late."

"Hold on now," said Big Momma. "We're not in that much of a hurry. Namesake, did you bring some things to wear for the program?" When I nodded, she smiled and said, "Then you will put them on. Excuse us, Shenetta. We'll be right back."

I got out of the car and followed her to the house. Bullet came in with us. Big Momma and I went into her bedroom, which always smelled like sassafras tea, Mum face cream, and talcum powder. She helped me out of my clothes and into the other ones, combed my hair, and even tried to give me finger curls at the end of my ponytail. Then she pushed two of her little ivory hair combs in my hair.

"Now you're spruced up, too, ain't ya, baby?"

Momma blew the car horn.

"Hush up," Big Momma said to the horn.

By the time we reached church, the parking lot was already loaded with cars and trucks. Momma pulled up in front of church and let us out. Argentina and the boys flew around to the Fellowship Hall door.

Inside, the sanctuary was packed, too. Big Momma and I waited in the back until Momma came in. The only space left was up near the front, which suited Big Momma fine. Momma, though, liked to sit near the back, by the door, so she could slip out if Rev. Walker got boring, or if they started to pass lots of collection plates. The only front seat I really wanted tonight, though, was up front by Big Momma's TV, watching Hillbilly Joe and Ozark Otto the Mountain Men take on Ivan and Igor the Russian Crushers.

We got ourselves squeezed into a small spot in the middle of a pew just before Miz Leggette, our Sunday School superintendent, stepped up to the main microphone and introduced Jamaica Washington as mistress of ceremonies. Jamaica is a senior at Gumbo Grove High School. She's Larry Washington's oldest sister. All us younger kids call her Miss Jamaica In-Charge because she loves to tell people what to do. She wins awards at the Elks' oratorical contests in Conway and Columbia almost every year and is on the school debating team.

Well, Jamaica gave a long, long, long welcome that made me yawn hard! Crunched up between Momma and Big Momma, I got hot, too. I managed to unbutton my coat, but I didn't dare try to take it off.

Jamaica asked us to stand for the invocation, and to stay standing for the Black National Anthem and processional. So we did. As soon as Rev. Walker finished the invocation, I slid out of my coat. What a relief!

Miz Wilhemena Birdsong banged down on the organ keys for the processional. The kids in the program marched in while we sang. The little kids in primary class came in first, dressed in white dresses and white shoes. They were followed by Antoine, Andrew, and the other younger boys, dressed in white, too. Pooch and the other guys in fourth, fifth, and sixth grades came next. They wore white, long-sleeved shirts and black ties, pants and shoes. Behind them were Hattie and them in white blouses and black skirts and shoes. They looked like penguins.

At first I felt left out because almost everybody I knew from school was in the program. But Momma hadn't been much on me being in anything after last year's Miss Ebony Calvary County Pageant that I was in. Boy, what a bummer that was! It was another reason why she was so upset about me being in the school play, and how was I going to act *this* time?

This is what happened. Near the end of the pageant, the emcee asked all the candidates questions. My question was, "What would you do if you caught your best friend cheating on a test?" They hadn't meant Hattie, of course. But our oldest sister, Arnetta, was caught cheating at Florida State earlier that same year, and got booted out of college. When I heard that question, I thought they meant I had to say something about her, or that they had heard about it, or something. I felt so awful, I didn't know what to say. I was so nervous, so . . . I started to cry. Momma said I was stupid to cry.

At the front of the church, kids stood in a line holding big red cardboard letters that spelled out Dr. King's name. They each said something about what the letter they held stood for. After each one spoke, Big Momma would smile and nod her head.

Jermaine Walker's older brother Dexter, a junior at Gumbo Grove High, came out next to give Dr. King's "I Have a Dream" speech. He shook his fist in the air, pointed his finger at us, and shouted. Everybody clapped hard.

"Didn't he do that well?" Big Momma said to Momma.

No wonder Jermaine was Dr. King in our Presidents Month play. He wouldn't have any problem learning that speech, I bet. I liked the program so far. Everybody sounded happy with what they were doing. They used words like "pride" and "success" and "win." I heard that word "slavery," too, but even it seemed to mean something that wasn't embarrassing, at least not tonight.

When Argentina walked out to stand by the organ, Big Momma, Momma, and I sat up straight. Argentina nodded at Miz Wilhemena, who began to plunk out the opening chords of "The Greatest Love of All."

Before she even finished the first stanza, Argentina had the folks warmed up and shouting. "Words so true!" somebody called out.

"Sing your song, child!" said somebody else.

She did have a good voice. People often asked her to sing at programs—that is, when they could run her down. Kids said she should try out for "Star Search" on TV, but she thought that was crazy. She just liked to sing, talk on the telephone, and hang out with Bunny and Big Boy.

I wish I could sing like that.

By now Argentina had pulled the microphone off the stand. She threw her head back, hit a high note and held it so long that we all broke out into clapping. "Do Jesus, that child can sing!" I heard people tell each other. When she finished, we gave her a standing ovation. Momma and Big Momma sat down last, nodding and smiling around at everybody.

Next came speeches about other famous Black folks. Some were the same ones in our school play. Big Head Jeff Thomas talked about Frederick Douglass. Jamaica In-Charge talked about how great Gumbo Dickson was, and how we should all be proud. Everybody said, "Amen!" to that.

I fell asleep against Big Momma's arm. When I woke up, I heard coins jingle. People were fumbling in their purses, pockets, and wallets. I heard Momma whisper to Big Momma that now was a good time to go.

All the kids in the program stood at the front of the church, facing us. "We are proud of Dr. Martin Luther King, Jr.," they said in unison. "May the Lord look upon this great leader with compassion. He was a Drum Major for Peace and Justice. Surely God has a place in heaven for him. He has a place in all our hearts. We are proud to be children of the Lord, and we are proud to be Afro-Americans."

After the program ended, I hurried with the other kids to Fellowship Hall for refreshments. "You all called yourselves Africans," I told Hattie when I got to her. Her plate was piled with cake and cookies.

"We said Afro-Americans. Nothing wrong with that," Hattie said.

"I was born in Gumbo Grove, South Carolina, in America, and there's nothing African about that," I said, puzzled.

"Are you quite sure about that?" Rev. Walker said behind me. He smiled at me. "Missed you in the program. Were you sick?"

"No, sir," I said, and felt stupid that he'd heard what I said to Hattie.

After we left church, Momma took Big Momma and me back to Cuffy's Island for the weekend. It was late when we got there. I was awake long enough to stagger inside the house, trip over Bullet, and fall asleep on the couch.

CHAPTER

SIX

On Monday morning back at school, Miz Vereen rang her bell to quiet us down. We didn't quiet down as fast as she wanted to, though, so she had to holler.

"We'll not have rowdiness this morning," she warned. "Otherwise you'll stay inside for recess. Understand?"

I sat up straight in my chair and nodded my head hard. I didn't want to get in trouble and it was only Monday. I hope she didn't get cranky. Sometimes she did, and boy, it was awful for us all day long!

Miz Vereen primped at her hair, then cleared her throat. "Now. I have a surprise. You'll simply love it, love it, love it."

"Is it food?" asked Bubba.

"Can we go home?" asked Carrot.

"I'm warning you!" She shook her finger at Bubba and Carrot. "Tomorrow and Wednesday we'll have two very special visitors in our room. They're storytellers from Baltimore, Maryland. A Mister . . . a Mister . . ." Miz Vereen peered down at her desk, moving her lips. Then she held up a piece of paper. "A Mister Yourself Kiwi, and a Miss . . . a Miss . . . unh, Minnie Africa. Yes, that's it, I guess. I can't read Miz T's handwriting."

We laughed at the funny-sounding names. I wrinkled up my nose at Hattie. Africa? Who'd want to have a last name like that? I figured Miz Vereen was joking again.

"After they tell you their stories, you'll have to write a story for them."

"Aw, do we have to?" Everybody groaned and moaned.

"Yes, you have to. But there'll be no spelling Tuesday and Wednesday. They're coming during language arts."

We cheered, clapped, and stomped our feet until Miz Vereen had to pound on her desk with a book and ring her bell again. We were like this a lot on Mondays. "Second warning! And we will have spelling today, so shush!"

I hated story writing. I had lots of ideas to write about, but Miz Vereen didn't let us write about what we wanted to. We usually had to write about our summer, or holiday vacations, or what we did over the weekend, or what the American flag meant to us. Over and over and over, until it got sooo boring!

Story writing meant hard spelling, too. There'd be lots of words I'd want to use because I knew what they meant. But Miz Vereen said we always had to stop and make sure we spelled each word right before we went any further. One time I had a cool idea about pretending I found a dinosaur skeleton when we visited Myrtle Beach State Park, but I couldn't spell dinosaur.

I couldn't find it in the dictionary, either. I wrote about a dog bone, instead, but I didn't like that story at all.

Miz Vereen made us put commas and periods in the right places as we went along, and everything had to be in real neat handwriting. That meant we had to copy, copy, copy what we wrote until she said it was neat and correct enough. My hand and my brain would be ready to pass out.

Our whole class did awful on storywriting, even the gifted and talented program kids Brandy, Kenyatta, Ernie, and Buffy.

I did like to listen to stories. It was easier than having to read them.

"And today, children, as you know, is the federal holiday for Dr. King," said Miz Vereen.

"How come we didn't get out of school today?" asked Hattie. "The schools over in Georgetown are closed, and in Columbia, too. This ole school is stupid for being open today."

Miz Vereen crossed her arms and frowned. I could tell she didn't like that crack about our school being stupid. "Young lady, you should be ashamed for calling your school names. The schools in our county are open because our school board says we are. Our school board chose to close for General Robert E. Lee's birthday. Many school districts across our great state choose to be closed for General Lee, even if this is a federal holiday. State's rights. General Lee was a great Confederate hero. It's part of our southern heritage to honor him in this way. Now you apologize for calling your school stupid."

Hattie mumbled that she was sorry, but I could tell that she really wasn't.

"Tell me something about Dr. King that you remember from the other day."

"He won some kind of prize for peace," said Buffy.

"He wanted to be a minister, like even when he was a child," I heard Hattie behind me say. Carrot and Pooch and some other kids said stuff, too.

"And he fought for people's civil rights," said Brandy.

I turned around and stared, surprised. Then I

raised my hand, eager to say something about him now, too, but Miz Vereen told me to put my hand down because we were ready to start writing.

"Now on a clean sheet of paper, I want you to write three paragraphs about what the Confederate flag and Dr. King mean to you. Be sure to write each word correctly, use your best handwriting, indent your paragraphs, and have a title."

Everybody groaned again, shuffled papers, and slammed desk tops. I knew the Confederate flag was on people's T-shirts and beach towels, and that some soldiers carried it during the Civil War. I bet she wanted me to write more than that. I didn't have any ideas about the flag and Dr. King together.

"Miz Vereen, how do you spell Confederate?" Pooch asked.

"Look it up, hon," Miz Vereen told him.

Pooch frowned and stuck out his lip. "Daggone, I'll be looking up that word all day."

I knew what he meant. All I had down was, Dr. King and the C.

"But like, why do we have to write about the Confederate flag on the Dr. King holiday?" asked Brandy.

"The flag is a symbol of our southern heritage and our history, don't you know," Miz Vereen told her.

"But what does the Confederate flag have

to do with Dr. King?" said Kenyatta, sounding puzzled.

Miz Vereen raised her eyebrows. "Oh, you Yankees. At least you, Brandy. Remember, girls, how we studied it when we discussed the U.S. Constitution in September? Oh, you girls hadn't moved here yet. No wonder! Because you two otherwise are so smart! Well, it has a lot to do with Dr. King. It stands for a way of life that we've held most dear, and for states' rights. That's why the War Between the States was fought, because the Yankees tried to take away our rights. Dr. King believed in rights for everybody. See the connection?"

"No," Brandy said slowly. "I thought the war was fought over slavery, too. Because the slaves wanted to be free but the people who owned them said they couldn't be, so everybody fought. Dr. King sure wouldn't have been in favor of slavery, would he?"

"Slavery had nothing whatsoever to do with the war." Miz Vereen had stopped smiling. One little pink dot stood out on each cheek. "The slaves were happy and content. They had everything they needed. They were brought from an uncivilized place to a civilized one."

I looked around. Hattie was frowning, with her chin stuck out. When she saw me looking at her she stopped frowning and shrugged her shoulders.

"Excuse me, Miz Vereen, but that's not what my mom said," said Kenyatta. "She told me that the slaves never wanted to be slaves, and that every chance they got they tried to get to freedom, and that Africa was just as civilized as America, in its own way."

Miz Vereen crossed her arms. "I beg your pardon?" she said in a snappy voice.

Boy, Miz Vereen was sure cranky! The room got as quiet as ice.

"I speak with authority, young lady. My great-great-grandfather Vereen owned Vereen's Plantation over in the Lime Hill section of our county. He had over fifty slaves, and all the slaves were happy. He fed them well. They hardly had to do any work at all. A man in Myrtle Beach wrote a marvelous book about Grandfather Vereen and how happy and comfortable his slaves were. They—"

"But, Miz Vereen," Kenyatta broke in, "if they were happy and comfortable, why did they still have to be slaves and wear chains?"

"Yeah, like that's totally weird, I mean totally," Brandy said. "Couldn't they have just worked for him and got paid?"

"You girls don't understand. When the war broke out, the Yankees came through. They burned Grandfather's beautiful home, killed his chickens, stole Grandmother's jewelry, and ran off all of his slaves, except for Mammy. She stayed right with us—I mean, right with them. She was loyal. The other ones that the Yankees ran off never did come back."

"They weren't run off, Miz Vereen, they left," said a voice from the doorway.

I jumped. It was Miz T. "If I might add something, Miz Vereen? Your great-great-grandfather must have forgotten to tell his slaves about freedom when he was supposed to because the Union soldiers didn't come through until two years after, and they told the slaves. When the slaves found out the truth, they left. That lady you called Mammy was Miz Katie Beecham. She stayed because she was paralyzed and couldn't walk. That's who Mt. Beecham Baptist Church is named after. Isn't that something? May I speak with you?"

"Is that right? I didn't know that," Miz Vereen said. "I hadn't heard that version before. My goodness. Well. You're sure about that?" She placed her fingers up against her throat for a second, then went to Miz T. "Just go ahead with your writing assignment," she said, "and keep quiet until I return."

As soon as she left, everybody started to talk and giggle low. When I turned around to say something to Hattie, I saw she was over to Kenyatta's desk. "Gimme five, girl. You sure told Miz Vereen."

"I hope I don't get in trouble," Kenyatta said.

"I like Miz Vereen. She's funny. I just didn't understand what she was talking about."

"Miz Vereen is sooo weird," Brandy giggled. "Doesn't she ever watch the 'Cosby Show'?" I saw her smile at Kenyatta. Kenyatta smiled back.

"Yeah, you did good, too, Brandy," I said, but I don't think she heard me because she didn't even look at me.

"I wouldn't ever want to have anybody be my slave," said Carrot.

"Hey man, I think it'd be cool," said Bubba. "And if that slave didn't do what I wanted, I'd get out my whip." He hunched his head and swung his arm around like he had a whip in his hand. "Pow! Pow! I'd beat 'em, just like on TV."

Ernie, Carrot, Hattie, and Pooch flew at Bubba. "Better shut your trap!" said Ernie.

"You're crazy, Bubba!" Hattie shouted.

"You be MY slave," said Pooch, "and let me beat on YOU. See if you like it!"

Bubba flung his arms in front of his face. "Hey, man, I was just joking, honest! Can't you take a joke?"

When Miz Nisby came in, everybody flew to their seats. She read us some stories that she called American Tall Tales. She told us some more about the storytellers coming, too. "Their names are Yusef Kwanzaa and Imani Afrika," she said.

"Miz Vereen called them something else," said Carrot. "Are these the same ones?"

"I'm sure they are," she said.

Bubba held up his hand. "Miz Vereen said we had to write about the Confederate flag and Dr. King. Do we still have to? And are we still gonna get recess?"

"Wait a minute, wait a minute, Miz Nisby," said Pooch. "I gotta ask you something first before you tell us if we gotta write or not. I hope you don't get mad with me like Miz Vereen did with Kenyatta and Brandy, okay? But wasn't slavery wrong? Miz Vereen said her granddaddy's slaves were happy and didn't hardly work."

"Oh dear, I'd rather not discuss what happened, since I wasn't in here. I'm just filling in for her now till she gets back. But I can certainly tell you that slavery was wrong."

Pooch and Libby told Miz Nisby what happened, anyway. But Miz Nisby said slavery was still wrong. Which meant Miz Vereen was wrong, too.

Miz Nisby leaned back against Miz Vereen's desk. "Children, the people who owned slaves in this country were caught up in making money the only way they knew how," she said. "Once they got started owning people they didn't know how to stop. Of course, some of them didn't want to stop. The owners depended on slaves for almost everything. They didn't want to give up their slaves so they told everybody that slaves weren't really people."

Miz Nisby said that the slaves did an incredible job building America and helping to make it what it is today. She said not to let anybody make us Black kids feel ashamed because some of our ancestors were African slaves. Then she said that nobody in the room should be ashamed of who they were, either.

"Some folks to this day try to make slavery sound like it was nice, fun, and normal, I guess like how you said Miz Vereen said. How could it be normal for one human being to own another? And if it was time for that slave to go to work he had to get up or be beaten—the women and children, too."

Miz Nisby went to the encyclopedia shelf and pulled out Volume Three. "Look. This is a cat-o'-nine-tails whip. It was a horrible weapon and caused a lot of pain."

Some of the kids gathered around close to look at the picture, and then looked at Bubba, whose face and ears turned almost purple, he was so embarrassed. For once I felt sorry for him. I stayed in my seat, though. I didn't want to see any awful whip.

"So Bubba, about your writing assignment. If Miz Vereen told you to write something, maybe you better do it. I don't know about recess. I will say this. Dr. King and thousands of Black people and white people, too, worked hard to change laws that kept Black people from being free. By helping to make Black people be free, Dr. King helped to make all people be free, including whites. I don't know how you can work the Confederate flag into all of that, but maybe you can."

At lunchtime, the only thing we talked about was what Miz Vereen and Miz Nisby told us. "Miz Nisby made more sense explaining slavery than Miz Vereen did," Lonnie Lee said between mouthfuls of her tuna sandwich.

"Well, I just wish nobody would talk about it at all," I said, but nobody heard me.

"Wonder what Miz T and Miz Vereen did back in the office?" said Bonnie Boo.

"Whatever it is they usually do when she goes," said Hattie. "This isn't the first time Miz T had to come get her about something. Boy, I didn't know she was gonna get so mad at me for saying school was stupid."

"Maybe Miz T will make her stay after school like she does us kids," Bonnie Boo giggled. "I see lots of teachers staying after school. You think it's 'cause they're bad, too? Was Miz Vereen alive when they had that War Between the States?"

"No, dummy," Lonnie Lee told her. "She's not that old. I heard her tell Miz Riley about what she was going to do when she hit forty-five."

We all went ohhh over that. Forty-five sounded old, old. Maybe it was her birthday and she felt real old. Maybe that's why she was cranky.

When we came back to our room after lunch Miz Vereen was there again, sitting at her desk, looking like she always did. She called us to attention like she always did, too. We did our afternoon work—like we always did. But we were extra quiet, and so was she. She didn't much smile, either. I figured she was mad at us.

But when she asked us to tell about our progress on our health projects, she didn't sound mad. She called on Brandy and Kenyatta, too, and smiled at them. They smiled back. Then I smiled at Miz Vereen, too. She smiled back. Finally everybody relaxed. We started to talk and whisper to each other, just like always.

The school bell rang. Miz Vereen lined us up and dismissed us. I hurried outside to try to catch up with Brandy, but I missed her again. When I looked back through the window into our room, Miz Vereen was standing by the globe and the American flag near her desk, looking real sad. I waved at her. When she saw me, she waved back, and smiled, just a little.

CHAPTER

SEVEN

I plopped down in my seat, breathing hard, and grinned at Hattie. "Beat you. I'm behind you only seven points now."

"Girl, you can't catch up with me," she said back. "I'm the number one ball player in town!"

I wiped my face on my shirt sleeve, and pushed my hair back with both hands. It was hot outside for January. We'd been playing a hard game of dodgeball, and I'd never got out.

Another thing. It was Tuesday, and time for the storytellers, but they hadn't arrived yet. I didn't want to write any stories today, but I sure did want to hear some. I wondered if she'd have long, blonde, brown, or black hair. Would he look like George Michael?

Suddenly I heard loud, jingly bells, like at Christmastime, and a tambourine, like the ones in church. And then a deep drum—taBOOM! Right outside our classroom door.

"What's going on?" Libby lisped.

Pooch snapped his fingers and bebopped. Miz Vereen stood up, smiling. "They're here, children, the storytellers!"

A dark-skinned Black lady wearing a long orange dress and an orange cloth wrapped around her head rolled in through our door like she was on wheels. She carried a tambourine in one hand. In her other hand was a long black, yellow, and blue piece of cloth that she swung all over the place. Behind her came a tall Black man with a thick, bushy beard wearing a green, silky bathrobe. He wore braids down to his shoulders under this funny little round yellow cap, and about a million necklaces, rings, and bracelets. He hit ta-BOOM on a red, black, and green drum strapped over his shoulder.

Embarrassed, I stuck my *Weekly Reader* up in front of my face, and squinched down in my seat. I'd never seen anything like this before. The kids were laughing and pointing. When I peeked around at Brandy, she was laughing, too. I wanted to go through the floor.

"Come alive, come alive, it's storytelling time!" the woman shouted as she rolled up to the front of the room. "We are with the National Association of Black Storytellers, and we're here to tell you stories!"

They stopped and smiled at us until Miz Vereen quieted everybody down. Then they began again:

We are storytellers, Black and proud!
Everybody, listen! Say it loud!

"Hey, they're doin' a rap!" yelled Pooch.

Listen long, and listen well
To the African stories we're about to tell!
Everybody clap now, clap, clap, clap!

They shouted, smiled, clapped, laughed, rang bells, and beat on that drum and tambourine till they finally got a few kids to clap. Well, Kenyatta and Ernie started it, then Hattie and Alicia Valendez and some others joined in. But I didn't.

I sneaked a peek at Brandy and Buffy. They were clapping, too! Well, I told myself, if they could do it, then it had to be okay. Relieved, I clapped a little.

The woman said something. It sounded like she said she had to borrow some gum. Hunh? I frowned up my nose at Hattie and giggled. She ignored me.

"I just spoke to you in an African language

called Ki-Swahili," the woman said. "I said Ha-BAR-ree GAH-nee. Say it, please. That means 'how are you?' My name is Imani Afrika. ee-MAW-nee. Say it, please. Imani is a Ki-Swahili word that means faith. My last name is Afrika, spelled with a k. That's my name because I'm proud that my ancestors came from the continent of Africa."

"And my name," said the man, "is Yusef Kwanzaa. Yusef means Joe. Kwanzaa is a Ki-Swahili word that means first. It's also a holiday, from December 26 to January 1. Kah-WAHN-zah. Say Kwanzaa, please."

I whispered his last name and her first name to myself. Was I really speaking African? The words sounded pretty. On TV in those old cartoons when they showed Africans speaking, all they ever said was "booga booga." I sat up a little more and listened harder.

The storyteller lady said she was happy we were saying African words, and that we should all be proud of who we were, no matter where we came from. When she started talking like that, I knew what she was going to talk about next—slavery! I hunched back down.

"The first story we're going to tell you is the story of Why Mosquitoes Buzz in People's Ears," she said. I sat up, surprised. "This is a story from West Africa. This is our interpretation of it."

Mr. Kwanzaa and Miz Imani told the story about how the way this crazy mosquito buzzed so much in folks' ears that the whole forest got turned upside down. That story was funny!

Miz Imani quickly pulled the cloth off her head, flipped it inside out and retied it into a purple turban. She unbuttoned the orange dress and let it drop to the floor. Under it was a silky purple gown. She looked just like a queen. She was so pretty that I had to grin wide.

When Miz Imani told us about a queen from Africa named Queen Nefer-something my eyes got wide. Did all African queens have jewels and lots of money and palaces like this Queen Nefer did? I thought kings and queens only lived in England and France. I thought there were only cannibals and monkeys and lions in Africa, like Miz Vereen said. I wanted to know more about this Nefer lady, but I was too scared to ask.

"And did you know," said Mr. Kwanzaa, "that certain Africans used to be able to fly?"

At first I thought he was making fun, like how they showed Black people in those old cartoons on TV looking like big, black, stupid crows.

"I was told this story when I was down at Beaufort, South Carolina," he said. "I talked with some storytellers named Ron and Natalie Daise, who had heard the story from people they knew. I read another version in a book by Virginia Hamilton. Now I'm going to tell it to you in my own way."

He closed his eyes for a second. Then he opened them and stretched wide his arms. "Long, long ago, a long, *long* time ago, there were people in America who were called slaves. These people had to work so very hard that it was almost too hard. These people had come from Africa. When many of these people who had come from Africa lived in Africa, they had been kings and queens and princesses, and farmers and merchants and healers.

"They were like that when they were forced to come to America, but nobody in America thought of them that way. In America they were thought of only as slaves, with no rights and no freedom and no history. These people wanted badly to go back home, to Africa.

"When they were stolen from their homes in Africa, they had had to leave behind their comfortable beds, their green gardens, their animals, most of their clothes, and all their friends. Very often they were separated from their husbands and wives and children, their grandparents and great-grandparents, aunts, uncles—everybody kin to them! Their master was mean and sometimes beat them. So they were very, very sad and very, very lonely.

"But in those days, some of these people also had a magic power that they had brought with them from Africa—inside their heads. One day some of them decided, 'Enough is enough! We are going back home, no matter what.' They said the magic words. They lifted their arms, their arms turned to wings, and they flew away. The master fussed and shouted, but there was nothing he could do. They flew away to freedom. Those folks had gone back home."

I thought about that story. It was happy and sad at the same time.

"I don't believe nobody can fly, except on a plane," said Bubba.

"Of course people can't fly," Buffy told him. "It's only a story."

Mr. Kwanzaa smiled. "You can go anywhere, in your mind. This story means that these people refused to be slaves. They had to be free, no matter what. So they flew back home in their minds—I think." He pointed his finger at us. "But have you ever heard someone say they moved so fast that they flew?"

"Oh yeah," we told him, nodding.

"Well, people fly in different ways."

Then they told us stories about Rumplestiltskin, the Man in the Seven League Boots, and Cinderella. "And now you're going to each write your own story," Miz Imani said.

We began to fuss.

"Don't worry. Spelling and punctuation don't count for right now. Just get your ideas down and make your story. You can correct your spelling and punctuation later."

"What?" we all asked.

"Miz Vereen says we have to spell every word correct as soon as we write it down," said Ernie.

"Shhh!" Lonnie Lee said. "Don't give Miz Afrika any ideas!"

"We all have important messages to give to the world, but often we don't have the time to look up the spellings right then," Miz Imani said. "So for now, just write any hard words down like how they sound to you. That way you can read them back to yourself when you're through the first time. That's what's important. Later you can go back and get your spelling and punctuation right."

That was the queerest thing I'd ever heard a teacher say, but it sure would help me write faster, I bet. I wouldn't forget what I wanted to write, either, trying to figure out how to spell some dang word.

Miz Imani said our story could be like Cinderella, but not with the same names. Or it could be like Queen Nefer, or Rumplestiltskin, or like that. She showed us how to write a simple story, too. "And be sure to use lots of description. Tell me what the object or person or animal or place looks like, smells like, might taste like, sounds like, and feels like to *you*, based on *your* opinion, okay?"

We all nodded, eager to get started. "So let's go." Miz Imani turned to Miz Vereen. "You will write with us, too, won't you?"

Miz Vereen said no thank you, because she had to grade her papers. Miz Imani handed her a sheet of writing paper anyway. "Thank you but no, dear, I'm a teacher," she said. "I don't need to write."

"I bet Miz Vereen can write a story, can't she, kids?" said Mr. Kwanzaa.

"Yeah!" we all yelled.

"You can help your students by letting them see you write, and see how enjoyable it is," said Mr. Kwanzaa. "I hear that you write plays."

Miz Vereen shook her head. "No, no. I was never good at writing. Well, I did dabble in theater in college back in Savannah. I did a little playwriting here, too, but they couldn't use it. Oh, all right, but I must spell each word correctly as I go."

"Of course," said Mr. Kwanzaa. He smiled wide at her and patted his beard. Miz Vereen smiled back so wide I thought her lips would come unhinged.

I tried to pin down one thing to write about. That was hard, because I had at least five ideas buzzing around in my head. Maybe I'd write about something pretty, like a princess who visits the wizard in the mountains. Or maybe about a unicorn that lived in the valley where rainbows grew. I glanced around to see what Brandy was doing. She and Kenyatta were whispering up a breeze. I frowned. Maybe I'd write about something creepy and ugly, like witches or Freddie Krueger, or ghosts. Maybe I'd write about Ole Green Alice, the witch. Remembering what Libby had called Hattie, and what Momma had called me, I decided that Ole Green Alice the witch would be black-skinned, and evil and ugly.

I looked back at Brandy again. She and Kenyatta were still jabbering. Why didn't Miz Vereen hear them and hush them up for talking, anyway? Who did that Kenyatta think she was? I was going to be Brandy's best friend, not her. I glanced back around, and then I began to write. Boy, my pencil was fired up *then*. I wrote that Ole Black Alice wore a stupid, ugly T-shirt just like the one that Kenyatta Threadgill was wearing, and wore her hair in ugly, long braids like Kenyatta Threadgill did. Then I threw in that she had crossed eyes and no teeth and a wart on the end of her nose, and had ugly Black skin.

The morning passed quickly. "It's time for us to go," said Miz Imani. "What a wonderful group you've been. Put your names on your stories, please."

Pleased with my story, I wrote down my name with lots of curlicues, like Argentina did.

"And pass them up to the front. After you work on them tomorrow, we'll read some aloud," she said.

Hand in? Read out loud?

Bubba poked papers against my back. I tried to stick my story under my notebook, but Miz Imani rolled over to me first with her hand out. Sick, I put my paper under the rest of the stories from my row, then handed them to her.

"Do we have to read 'em out loud?" I whispered.

"We'll see." When Miz Imani bent close to me for a second, I could smell her. She smelled like cinnamon. Her dark skin was the same color as mine, but hers looked as smooth as glass. She had dimples, too. "And what is your name, little sister?" she asked.

Hattie, Mary Inside said.

"Mary Elouise," I said real low.

"Very pretty name," she said. "Very dignified."

My face got hot. I sure didn't feel dignified. I frowned up at her.

"Names are very important," Miz Imani explained to the class. "They help to tell everybody who you really are."

Kenyatta raised her hand. "I know what my

name means. It means Kenya, which is the name of a country in Africa."

"African," Jamal snickered. "You're an African, too. Bet you came from Africa."

"Why not? That's a wonderful continent to come from," said Mr. Kwanzaa. He pulled down the map of the world and showed us where Africa was, and where Kenya was. "We visit lots of African countries."

"Do you see cannibals or naked people in Africa?" Pooch asked.

"Pooch, don't ask people embarrassing questions!" Libby hissed.

"Oh, that's not embarrassing," Mr. Kwanzaa said, "because we don't see any cannibals when we visit Africa. What's a cannibal? And guess what? We don't see any more naked people in Africa than what you see at the beach here in Gumbo Grove. If you read about the African countries, especially Ghana and western Africa, you'll learn a lot. You'll find out about lots of everyday things and foods right here that came from Africa. That's where many of your ancestors came from, too."

"Did mine come from there?" asked Bonnie Boo.

Everybody laughed, even Mr. Kwanzaa. Then he winked and smiled. "You never know." He gathered up the remaining papers and put them in a bag he carried around his other shoulder. I wanted to bite myself for writing that stupid story. What if Miz Thomas or Miz Stokes—or Momma!—found out? I could get killed.

Mr. Kwanzaa and Miz Imani began to sing, clap, shake bells, and hit the tambourine again. This time we all clapped, even me. I halfway hoped Mr. Kwanzaa would lose his bag before they came back.

"Now THAT was fun," said Lonnie Lee afterwards. "Bonnie Boo, you dip head! Don't you remember Momma saying our great-grandparents came from Germany?"

"About scared me half to death when they came in, though," I said. "All that jumping and hollering and beating on drums like they were crazy."

"What do you mean? They were singing!" said Lonnie Lee. "Didn't you like them? She was pretty. He was cute, too."

"They were okay." I shrugged. I looked around at Brandy. Now her feet were on Kenyatta's chair rung. She was clapping hands with Kenyatta and singing the storytellers' song. I frowned. Kenyatta again! Suddenly I didn't care if she did find out about my story. Maybe I'd even read it out loud tomorrow.

But I got an awful thought. If that story got read out loud, Brandy would hear it, too, and maybe get mad at me because she'd know I was writing awful stuff about Kenyatta. In fact, probably everybody would. And how would Kenyatta feel? She'd never done anything mean to me. Big Momma would say I was being jealous over Kenyatta and Brandy being friends. I slumped down in my chair. What was I going to do?

After school Hattie and Maizell walked home with me. "Boy, those storytellers had me coming and going," Hattie said. "That mosquito was something else, too. Buzzz! What'd you write about? I wrote about a bear that turned into a fly and ate all the honey he wanted."

"My story? Well, I wrote—Hattie, I think I'm gonna get in big trouble. I wrote a bunch of nasty stuff about Kenyatta. I even used words that you did when you got mad."

"Yeah? Like what?"

I told her my story. She giggled all through it, then she put on a real sad face. "Yes, girl, you're in big trouble. I'll come to your funeral, for true, 'cause face it, if your momma or Miz Thomas find out, you're gonna die." She shook her head like I was already buried in the ground. "It definitely is not my fault though, because I did not tell you to write that story. Maizell's a witness, aren't you?"

"Hunh?" Maizell said. "What?"

"Mary Elouise, why'd you write that stuff?"

"I don't know," I said. "Yes, I do. I don't like

how Kenyatta's always up in Brandy's face. Always talking and laughing—"

"Brandy? Then you oughta get in trouble." Hattie walked fast and stiff-legged up the street. Maizell hurried after her.

"Hattie!" I ran after her. "I gotta do something about my story!"

"Ask Brandy!" she shot back.

"No, I want you to help me! You always know what to do. Wait up!"

Well, that did the trick. She slowed down so I could catch up with her. "Can't we get the story back and change it?" I begged.

"We who?" she snapped. She didn't say another word until we got to our houses. "I'll think about it. Bye."

Needing some relief, I popped inside the house and went straight for the TV set. I was just in time for "Barbie's Adventures."

I liked using the pillowcase for hair last time. Thinking of it, I remembered Miz Imani and her scarves and turbans. And you know what? Her hair was cut as short as Pooch's! I knew because I saw her head when she pulled that turban off. She looked like a peanut head. Maybe she kept scarves on because she couldn't grow hair.

Now where was "Barbie's Adventures"? I punched the remote-control buttons. What I saw was a Black man, woman, and little girl drifting on a raft in the ocean. Then the scene shifted to this same girl, older now, going to school. She was in airplanes and ships, then driving fast cars. Suddenly this same girl was grown and had her hands on her hips, smiling right into the camera at me.

Barbie, Pammie, and Tammie danced up to this Black kid and put their arms around her. Barbie said, "Welcome home, Keisha."

"Welcome home who? You?" I asked the TV.

"Now Keisha can help us continue to fight for justice," Tammie said. "Keisha can join us in all our new adventures."

The scene turned blue. The words "Barbie's *New* Adventures" popped on the screen. In the middle of the theme song a voice announced, "Featuring Barbie, Tammie, Pammie, and Keisha!"

The three of them—and HER—bounced across the screen. Amazed, I clapped my hand across my mouth. And where was their hair? They all had short, curly hair and big hoop earrings, just like this Keisha kid did! Baldies! "What are you doing to my show?" I shook my fist at the TV, then punched to another channel. My favorite program ruined by this Keisha kid!

But while I fussed, I became so curious about what this Keisha would do that I flipped back to the program. There she was, dancing and singing right along with them. Her voice was halfway decent, I guess. She had her own guitar, too. Just then Andrew and Antoine came in.

"No, we can't watch this!" Antoine said. Snatching the remote control out of my hand, he turned it to the "Transformers."

"That's okay; I'm not watching it, either," I said.

That made Andrew turn back to it. "Who's this kid?" he asked, pointing at Keisha. "She's cute." They watched the show all the way through. So did I.

"I like this new show better," Andrew said. "Now it's got some soul!"

I liked it, too, but I didn't tell them.

CHAPTER

EIGHT

Where in the world were my narrator papers? I had to practice!

For the last two hours, I'd been looking for them. By now I had practically torn our house apart. I even peeped in Andrew and Antoine's room. When I roared through the kitchen, jerking out drawers and flinging open cabinets—*still* looking for them—Momma stopped me.

"Child, whatever are you trying to find?" she asked. "Your play papers?" She cleared her throat. "Well, I know you *will* find them, won't you?"

"Oh yeah, Momma, they're right around here somewhere. I'll find them in a minute."

"I know you will. And I know you won't stop looking until you do."

Well, I looked and I looked until I thought my eyes would drop out. No papers. I crumpled up in our big old blue armchair in the corner and sniffled.

Argentina stuck her head around the corner of the wall and stared at me. "You're giving me a headache snorting and sighing so much. I can't even hear the TV. Isn't your nose tired? Aren't your lungs sore?"

"Quit teasing, Argentina," said Momma. "Remember, you promised you'd behave. Mary Elouise, find those papers."

"Momma, I've been trying, and I can't find them!"

Argentina sat down on the armchair beside me and didn't say anything for a little while. Then she pecked me on the arm. "Did you look in the car?"

"No!" I flew out that door to the car. Scrunched up between the bottom of the seat and the floor were my papers, right where I'd left them from the first rehearsal. I straightened out the sheets as carefully as I could, and brushed the mud and sand off them.

"I got them, I got them!" I bounced back into the house. Momma just nodded her head.

"Good. You owe me one, chile." Argentina winked at me slyly, then plopped down on the couch in front of the TV.

But when I started to read my part, I almost

wished I hadn't found it. It read like Miz Vereen had written it, with big, long words that I couldn't even understand.

"Argentina, can you help me?"

"Later maybe."

"Momma, can you?"

"Sugar, I'll try. You know I'm not real good at this. What's wrong?"

She had trouble reading it, too. She gave up and went on to her night job. I struggled on. Then I remembered my awful story about Ole Black Alice. So I worried over that for a while. What was I going to do? Then I tried to go back to concentrate on my part. What did "impoverished" mean? How did you pronounce s-i-g-n-i-f-i-c-a-n-t?

Boy, what a mess. Suddenly I remembered Mr. Kwanzaa's story. I wished I could grow wings right now and fly away, too. But I couldn't, so I did the next best thing: I went to sleep, right in the old armchair. Argentina had to wake me up and drag me to bed.

The next morning almost as soon as school started Miz Vereen had us line up for rehearsal. I stood by Brandy again. "I bet you get to wear a real pretty dress playing Miz Washington, hunh," I said to her.

"I don't know," she said.

I shot a look at Kenyatta and felt proud that Brandy and I were talking—until I remembered my story again. Oh geez! I edged out of line and flew over to Hattie. "What are we gonna do about my story?" I whispered.

"I don't know what WE are gonna do, but YOU better do something."

"Like what?"

"Like ask Miz Imani for your story back."

"I can't do that. If she hasn't read it yet, and if I ask her, then she'll read it. And boy, I'll be in it deep then."

"Well, maybe find out first if she's read all the papers, and if she hasn't, then get Mr. Kwanzaa's bag, take out your story, change it, and put it back."

The cafeteria was noisy when we got there. Miz Imani sat at one of the tables with Mr. Kwanzaa's bag beside her. She wore huge silver earrings that came down to her shoulders, a long blue dress, a red shawl, and sandals. She didn't have anything on her head this time, and check this out: She didn't have more than two inches of hair on her whole head!

"Hattie, look! Miz Imani is a baldie! Look! No hair!"

Kenyatta, who was walking past, heard me. "Oh, Mary Elouise, lots of women wear their hair short on purpose. Haven't you ever seen Afro hairstyles before? I think they're sharp." She and Yolanda walked over to Miz Imani, where a crowd of kids were gathering.

"Shoot, she needs a wig." I wrinkled up my nose at Hattie.

"You better be worrying about your story and leave Miz Imani's hair alone," Hattie said loudly, then whispered, "and quit talking so ignorant." She went over to Miz Imani. Brandy was there, too, talking to Kenyatta.

I thumped down on a seat and cut my eyes at Kenyatta. She wouldn't be so Miss Know Everything if she read my story! Whoo, I sure know I didn't mean what I just thought. I had to get that thing back, but how? I didn't really want to do what Hattie suggested. That would be stealing, wouldn't it? The storytellers would be coming to our class after play practice. I beat my fists against my head. I wasn't acting ignorant doing that, either. I was desperate!

At play practice George Dozier, the narrator for the Presidents Month section, started things off. He talked about George Washington being the father of our country and our first president. "George Washington wore a white wig," he said. We all thought that was funny and laughed.

"And he also wore false teeth," George began to laugh, too, "made out of hippo bone—" he dropped his papers, giggling, "and wood." George giggled so hard he couldn't stop. We couldn't either. Miz Riley had to hush us up.

The kid who played Thomas Jefferson

coughed, snorted, and sneezed his part so much that nobody understood him. Larry Washington, who played Ben Franklin, read so quietly that Miz Riley had to ask him three times to repeat his part.

Brandy was the only one in the first section who said her lines right. In fact, she'd even memorized them. Miz Riley congratulated her.

The Valentine skit was a blowout. Cupid mixed up his lines. Aaron, the puppy, acted such a fool barking that everybody went into giggles, including Kasheba, the kitten. Even Kimiko, who was the Love Month narrator, had problems.

The Black History segment was next. Miz Riley motioned us to come to the stage. Oh boy. I dragged myself up there and lined up with the other kids across the side of the stage. She told me to start.

"Africans first came to American shores," I began. Just then something tickled my throat, making me choke. Kids started to laugh. I was embarrassed. I wasn't trying to be funny. I coughed some more and stumbled over my words.

"Go get a drink of water, hon," said Miz Vereen. "Use the backstage water fountain."

I rushed backstage, gulped down a mouthful of water, and tried again. I also introduced famous people, who talked about who they were.

"And next is Kenyatta Threadgill," I read, "por-por—"

"Portraying," said Miz Riley.

"—portraying the part of So-So-So—"

"Sojourner Truth."

"So-So-So—"

"SO JER NER," said Miz Riley.

My mouth still wouldn't act right.

"Mary Elouise's not even trying," I heard Libby say from the chorus section. "Told you I shoulda got that part."

"Kenyatta, say your lines, please," said Miz Riley.

Kenyatta walked over to me, empty-handed.

"Where's your papers?" I whispered. "Forgot 'em, I bet."

"I'm going to try without them," she whispered back. "I am Sojourner Truth," she began. "I believe in freedom for my people. I also believe in women's rights. One of my speeches about women's rights later became famous. It was called my 'Ain't I a Woman' speech."

But when Kenyatta began to recite "Ain't I a Woman" wearing overalls, a T-shirt, and high-tops, I had to giggle. She sure didn't look like a woman to me! The more she spoke, the more I giggled.

Miz Thomas gave me a dirty look. "Good work, Kenyatta," she said. "I wish everyone was as interested in their parts as you and Brandy are."

"Thanks," Kenyatta said. "We got together this weekend and studied."

My face flamed, and I pressed my lips together. When my part was over, I sat back down at a table by myself and felt low. It looked like Kenyatta was stealing Brandy away from me. Nothing was going right for me anymore. I couldn't even get my words straight. I didn't see any reason now for me to even be in this stupid play.

And I still had to do something about that story!

Hattie sat down beside me. "I'm glad my part rhymes," she said. "You got a bunch of rough ole big words in yours."

I was grateful for that. "I felt so stupid up there, Hattie. Everything's going wrong. Why did I ever want to be in this dumb play?"

"Don't give up yet," she said. "This was just the first practice. You'll get better. I got an idea about your story, too. Bend down like you gotta tie your shoe and listen to me. Miz Imani's got the stories in that bag. I know because I asked. She said she hadn't read all of ours yet, 'cause they had the other fourth-grade classes' papers to read. I know 'cause I asked about that, too. She said she was gonna read ours in the lounge before they come to our class. Maybe while she's in there we can get Mr. Kwanzaa's bag or you can just ask her for your story."

"We can't go in the lounge," I said.

"Maybe she meant the library lounge. She

can sit in the library and read and rest. That's where she was yesterday."

I was surprised. Teachers had little hiding places all over school. I never thought about a library being like a lounge where you just sat around and rested.

"Did she say whether she had read my story?" I asked.

Hattie slapped her forehead with her hand. "That's what I forgot to ask."

I saw Miz Imani stand up with the bag and walk out of the cafeteria. "There she goes," said Hattie. "So what are you gonna do?"

"I don't know, but whatever it is, will you do it with me?"

Hattie rubbed her nose, frowned, then shrugged and grinned. "Okay. Whatever you're gonna do, girl, you better hurry up and do it—or wait till class."

It was now or never. I had to get my story back before class, no matter what. "But how do we get out of here?"

"Let's meet in the hall. Tell Miz Riley you got to go to the bathroom. I'll ask Miz Vereen for me." She strutted over to Miz Vereen.

I raised my hand. "Miz Riley?"

Hattie and I reached each other in the hallway just in time to see Miz Imani go into the teachers' lounge.

"Maybe she's just gonna come right back out," I said. "Let's wait a little."

"But maybe this is the lounge she means," Hattie said.

I bit my lip. "Oh. You go in first."

"Okay, but *I'm* not touching NOBODY's bag, hear? You're gonna have to get the story or ask her for it."

Slowly Hattie opened the door. She peeked in, then walked into the lounge, and I followed. I'd never been in the teachers' lounge before. I thought it would just have a row of toilets and a washbowl, like our girls bathroom had. But it looked like a whole house in one room. On one side along the wall were a kitchen sink, a green refrigerator, a microwave oven, a big coffee pot, a pop machine, and a snack machine. Against another wall were a copy machine, a stencil machine, a TV set, and a big yellow poster on a bulletin board that said, "CLEANLINESS IS TEACHERLY."

Some magazines, a couple of bottles of aspirin, and some other medicine sat on a glass coffee table in front of a big brown couch. Also on the table was Mr. Kwanzaa's bag. Hattie pushed me toward it.

Should I wait for Miz Imani to come out of the toilet? If I opened the bag and took out my story, would I be stealing? I'd never done anything like this before. If I got caught, would I go to jail?

"Mary Elouise, do something!" Hattie hissed.

Gritting my teeth, I edged over to the bag and touched it. Well, the world didn't end. I unbuckled the straps and fumbled through papers until I found our class's folder. This wasn't hard to do at all. As I went through the papers, I noticed some titles of other kids' stories. There was Ernie's: "The Big Red Eye." And Bubba's: "The Giant Roach That Became a Car." I wondered what Brandy had written about.

"Mary Elouise," Hattie whispered, "you better hurry and—"

The restroom door opened and Miz Imani walked out.

At first she looked surprised to see us. Then she saw my hands in her bag. "Excuse me? Do you need something in there?"

"I . . . I . . . I . . ." My voice drained away down my throat.

Miz Imani took the bag. "You're Mary Elouise, aren't you?"

I couldn't say a word.

"Yes m'am, that's her," said Hattie. "She didn't mean any harm, Miz Imani, m'am. She just wanted to work on her story some—"

"And you're Hattie, aren't you?"

Hattie shut up, too.

"Let me find your story, okay?" She sat down on the couch and fiddled with the bag. Then she paused. "You don't go into people's bags without permission. Didn't you know that?"

I nodded. I felt awful inside. Miz Imani pulled out our class's folder that I had rumbled through and neatened up the pages.

"Ole Black Alice?" she asked.

My voice came back. Oh, don't read it! "Yes, m'am. Can I have it back, please? I didn't mean to get into your bag, m'am. I won't ever do it again. I'm sorry. I just wanted my story."

"This story must be very important to you," she said. "Come sit by me."

I edged over to her, but I didn't sit down. When I looked down at her, I could see her scalp through her short hair.

"Do you like to write?" she asked.

I'd been so busy staring I didn't hear her. "Hunh?"

"Mary Elouise!" Hattie said. "No, m'am, she hates to write."

"I see." Miz Imani shook her head. "Mary Elouise, I bet I look strange to you with my long dresses, and my short Afro."

She dropped my story in her lap and rested her hands on it. "Sit down, please, girls, for a second."

"Oh no, thank you, m'am," said Hattie, reaching for the doorknob. "We gotta get back to the cafeteria."

Miz Imani patted the couch and cleared her throat, meaningfully. "I said, sit down, girls."

Boy, we hopped to that couch quick then.

"I used to have thick, straight hair down to my waist," she said, "and I was so proud of it that I'd stay at the beauty shop for hours getting every kind of thing done to make it straighter, just like in the pictures in *Ebony* magazine and *Essence* and on TV."

"Oh lucky!" I said.

She shook her head, and her big earrings jangled. "But at the same time I got to be so vain about it that I was mean to my friends. I bragged about how much money I spent trying to get it so straight that it would blow in the air. I was so involved with my hair that I wouldn't take time to play baseball or dance or go bike riding or anything. Didn't want to get that fine hair dirty or messy or kinky one little bit, you understand. Sometimes I even pretended I had blonde hair, blue eyes, and real light skin."

What? She did that, too? I didn't think anybody did that but me. I wanted to ask her why she used to feel that way. I know why I do.

"This sounds just like you, Mary Elouise," said Hattie.

"Oh, it doesn't!" I said quickly. My face burned, though.

"Well, it's just what some folks go through

sometimes." Miz Imani looked at me. "*I* didn't know any better, and I went overboard. I was what the old people called 'color struck.' I thought I had to have rich friends, too. I wasn't very happy inside, though, because I was always chasing after rich kids. I had to learn to stop thinking the words Black or brown or yellow or African-American meant bad, dirty, and ugly. I had to start thinking of them as good, clean, and pretty."

I shrank down. This woman was reading my mind. I tried changing the subject. "Are you a real African?"

"I said African-American, which means my ancestors came from Africa, just like yours did."

"I ain't African," I said. "I was born in South Carolina."

Miz Imani laughed. "You are an American of African ancestry, born in South Carolina—just like me! You will always have your African heritage. Be proud of it."

"I wish you could meet my big sister Raisin," Hattie put in. "She knows all about stuff like this, too."

Miz Imani told us she was born Tywanna Bishop on Turner's Isle, that little island on the other side of Cuffy's Island. Her family moved to Atlanta when she was in high school. She attended Spelman College there. She changed her name legally to Imani Afrika and cut her hair short after she saw how pretty and happy the other Black women students were who had short Afros and knew about their African heritage. The women who did that were light-skinned and dark-skinned both. She said that being light-skinned or dark-skinned didn't matter, because you were still Black, that it was something to be proud of, and that one shade of color was just as pretty as another.

I still wasn't so sure about that. All I saw in the videos on TV were light-skinned Black dancers and singers with long, long hair. I never saw anybody my color.

She stopped suddenly and looked at us with her big, brown eyes. She seemed so friendly. "Mary Elouise, tell me more about Ole Black Alice, the witch."

My mouth froze up again.

"Oh, her?" Hattie said bravely. "Oh, she's just a Halloween witch, nothing special."

Miz Imani ignored Hattie. "Mary Elouise, tell me more about Ole Black Alice, the witch. I remember hearing a story about a *green* witch. Miz Thomas told me about her."

Miz Thomas! I hunched down. Did she show my story to HER? She'd tell Momma for sure. "I unh, well, she's like her, yeah. I just made a few changes."

"Were those changes based on a real person?" Miz Imani asked.

Say no! said Mary Inside. I started to say no, but when I glanced at Miz Imani, I knew I'd have to tell her the truth. She was too nice to lie to. So I nodded. "At Gumbo Grove Elementary?" she asked. I nodded again. "Someone in your class?" Yes.

"Does this person look or act like the way you described her?"

"No. Miz Imani, I don't want to read it out loud, please. It was just something stupid I did. I made up a lot of stuff just out of my head. Ole Black Alice is just somebody in my head, okay? I don't want anybody to see my story, please."

"No one's seen it except me. And no, you don't have to read it out loud. I'll give it back to you in class." Miz Imani looked at her watch, then stood up. "I've enjoyed our little talk. Mary Elouise and Hattie, I'm going to give something very special to you both when I come to class, okay?"

Hattie looked greedy. "Can you give us a hint?"

"You'll have to wait. And, Mary Elouise? You tell Ole Black Alice that you don't have to have long hair or blue eyes or light skin to be pretty. Remember that I said that dark skin is pretty, too, just like yours is."

I giggled when she told us that. I hadn't heard people ever say that Black was pretty unless they were talking about their car or a dress. Nobody had ever said that I was pretty, either, except Big Momma.

Miz Imani was sure pretty, though. And, of course, Big Momma was!

"Tell her to use her brains and common sense and what's inside of her, too," Miz Imani added.

"Yes m'am. Bye." We flew out that door.

"Whew, I'm glad she wasn't mad," I said as we hurried back. "But wasn't it funny when she said we were pretty?"

"Shoot, I've been knowing that I'm pretty," Hattie said back.

After we got back to the cafeteria, I wondered why the teachers didn't ask how come we'd been gone so long. Then I saw why. The clock showed we'd been gone less than fifteen minutes. It seemed like hours. I thought about what Miz Imani had told us. I decided that I liked her a lot. A whole lot.

Jermaine Walker came over and sat down beside me. "You still wanna swap your part? I sure don't want mine," he said.

I shook my head. "I'm stuck with mine now. You got Dr. King. Dexter just did it in church."

"Everybody thinks I can do it 'cause Dexter did. But I can't even pronounce half the words. I hate to get up in front of people. I hate to be in programs!"

"I know what you mean. I really wanted to be

in this at first, but now I don't know. Maybe Dexter can help you."

"I don't wanna ask, though." He stuck his hands in his pockets. "Well, see ya."

When I looked behind me, I saw Brandy, Kenyatta, Yolanda, and Ashley sitting together. I shot a mean look at Kenyatta.

But she only said, "Hey Mary Elouise, come sit with us."

I jumped up. "Okay." I squeezed in close between her and Brandy.

"Eeek, she's gonna play with my hair! You are sooo weird!" Brandy slid away from me while Ashley and Yolanda laughed.

"Never mind." Embarrassed, I went back to my table. Why didn't she like me? I was doing everything I could to make her like me, but all she did was laugh and call me names. I wondered if Kenyatta was saying mean things to her about me to make her act that way. But Kenyatta never said anything mean about anybody.

Kenyatta followed me. "You coulda stayed. Don't pay any attention to Brandy, Mary Elouise," she said. "She can be an airhead sometimes. Come on back."

I shook my head. She went back to her giggling table.

As soon as rehearsal was over and we were

back in our classroom, Miz Imani and Mr. Kwanzaa came in banging that drum and that tambourine.

Mr. Kwanzaa told us how much they liked our stories. He began to pass them back and discuss them. I held my breath. But Miz Imani came to my desk with my story in her hand. "I made some suggestions as to how you could still write about Alice the witch."

When she handed the paper to me I had to fight to keep from snatching it out of her hand and tearing it up into a billion pieces right then and there. "Maybe you could keep her green. You see a lot more green witch masks at Halloween than black ones, don't you?"

"Oh, yes, m'am." I'd have said yes to anything right now.

Miz Imani, though, told me to come with her to the back of the room and talk more about it. I followed her to the table where Rambo I and Rambo II, our pet gerbils, sat in their cage.

"Have you ever read stories about Black people that made you feel embarrassed?" she asked. "Did those stories make you think Black people were nasty or stupid?"

I nodded.

"Then why would you write a story like that, too?"

"I don't know," I said. Then I sighed, "Well, I was mad at a girl."

"Maybe the people who wrote some of those other stories were mad, too, and just wrote mean, wrong things because that's how they wanted Black people to be, even if it wasn't true. What do you think?"

"I hadn't thought about it that way." I sure didn't want to be like that, either.

"Well, try it again. You don't want to hurt anybody when you write. When you try to do wrong to somebody else, sometimes it comes back on you, and you get hurt yourself."

Yeah, like almost getting in BIG trouble for going through Mr. Kwanzaa's bag to get that story, I thought.

Miz Imani stood up. "I'll be right back." She went over to Hattie. When they came back, she gave us a book called *African Kings, Queens, Heroes and Heroines of the World*. "Since you two seem to be such good friends—I noticed how Hattie spoke up for you this morning, Mary Elouise—I'm giving you both this book. I'm giving it to you both because I want you to share it. I hope you enjoy it."

I thanked her, but I was disappointed. I thought she'd give us some money or a bracelet. Hattie looked disappointed, too. She took the book and handed it to me. I saw Miz Imani's name on the cover. "You wrote this whole thing yourself?" I asked, surprised.

Miz Imani nodded. "Look inside." In big swirling letters she had written, "To Mary Elouise Avery, and to Hattie Stackhouse, two pretty African-American princesses who will one day be Royal Queens."

My mouth fell open. Hattie giggled. "Hey, look at my name, how you wrote it, Miz Imani! Wow! Can I hold it, Mary Elouise? It's half mine, too, you know."

I handed it to her. "Thank you, Miz Imani." I meant it this time.

The storytellers gave presents out to everybody, but I noticed that nobody else got a book like ours.

And guess what? When Miz Imani and Mr. Kwanzaa left, some of the kids came around to see what Miz Imani had given to me. Brandy even came over.

"That is just totally incredible, that *you* have a book signed by a famous writer," she said.

"So do I," said Hattie. "It's fifty percent mine, and my name is in there, too."

Pooch read the inside of the book. "She wrote that Mary Elouise and Hattie were pretty!" he laughed. "Ohh, Miz Imani must be blind!"

"Shut up, Pooch!" Hattie doubled up her fist.

"Mary Elouise, you're famous, at least for our class, and Hattie, too, to get a book signed like that," said Kenyatta.

Everybody nodded, even Brandy!

Boy, did that make me feel tall. I grinned at Brandy as big and wide as I could.

"So who gets to hold the book first?" Hattie asked. "I wanna show Raisin and everybody."

"Well, I wanna show Momma and Argentina and Big Momma."

"I know!" Hattie snapped her fingers. "Let's go to my house right after school and look at it together. Momma and Raisin'll be home pretty soon and we can show it to them. Then you can take it home and show it to your folks. We can go back and forth."

That sounded like a good idea to me. I gave the book to her and she stuck it in her desk. I got up my nerve and went over to Brandy. Since she thought I was so totally incredible, maybe things were starting to look up. "Can I sit by you at lunch? I promise I won't mess with your hair or squeeze in like I did."

Brandy shook her head. "I'm sitting with Buffy, Ashley, Yolanda, and Kenyatta today," she said.

"Oh." Disappointed, I ate lunch with Hattie, who sat by Lonnie Lee and Bonnie Boo, who sat across from Yolanda and Kenyatta, who sat by Buffy, Ashley and you-know-who. I thought about talking about Miz Imani's book to try to get Brandy to talk to me, but I changed my mind. These things took time, I told myself.

But Mary Inside said back, How much longer is it gonna take to be friends with this kid Brandy? Twenty years?

CHAPTER

NINE

It was Friday. I was going to Big Momma's for the weekend again. We had a lot to talk about, for true!

We turned off Strom Thurmond Highway, and bumped across the wooden bridge over Dog Leg Swash. This end of Gumbo Grove didn't have motels, condos, amusement rides, and beachwear shops. It had tobacco fields, swamps, firecracker shops, mobile homes, and little wood houses. Miz Prieleu, one of Big Momma's best friends, lived out here. They were both members of a local chapter of the Order of Eastern Star. Miz Prieleu's house was green, with a tin roof. It set right by the highway where it curved toward Sigmon's Creek. Maddog Frank, her bull, was staked out on the strip of grass between the two lanes. We waved at him as we went past. He was a grouchy, mean old thing.

We shot across the drawbridge onto Turner's Isle, where Miz Imani said she was born. I wondered if there was a big sign somewhere saying, "Home of Famous Storyteller" or something. I didn't see any. I guess signs like that were only for movie stars and baseball players.

Anyway, I hardly saw any tourists out this way. I was glad. Tourists like to stare and point their fingers at us local folks. Sometimes they stop in the middle of Fifteenth Street, come right in our yards, and try to take pictures of us.

We drove down to Montegue's Ferry Boat Landing located at the edge of the Big Sing River. Mr. Isaiah Montegue owned the ferry. He waved us onto the front of his boat, and pushed wooden blocks behind each tire on our car so it wouldn't move around. Mr. Montegue liked to visit Big Momma. He brought her presents and took her places. I think he was her boyfriend. He was bald-headed, smoked a pipe, and had a big, thick moustache.

Mr. Montegue revved up the motor, and his little white ferry slid out into the water. The Big Sing emptied into the ocean right here. Today the ocean was rough, so the river was, too. Phooey. The waves slapped against the sides of the ferry and sent streams of water rolling under our car. With the water so rough, we'd be forever crossing over to Cuffy's Island, even though it was only three miles away.

Mr. Montegue's ferry rocked to the left, taking us high in the air. It rocked to the right, bringing us low to the water. My stomach rocked with it.

"Argentina," Momma was saying, "don't you run off when we get to Big Momma's. I want you to help me and Mary Elouise wash clothes."

Argentina had been snapping her fingers and singing to a song on Andrew's boom box. At the words "wash clothes" she froze. "But, Momma—"

"That way we can finish quicker, and I can get back home with you before it's too late," Momma went on. "I don't like being on this ferry at night when the water's carrying on like this.

"Children, Big Momma's down sick again. Lord knows I don't know what it is this time. Andrew and Antoine, please remember that Big Momma's sick. Don't act wild and be loud. Clean up her garden, which you were supposed to have done last fall. Mary Elouise, don't keep Big Momma up all night playing checkers. Everybody hear me?"

We all said yes.

"What's wrong with Big Momma?" I asked. She'd sounded all right the last time I talked with her.

"Oh, everything's acting up again. Might be that same cold or it might be the flu," Momma said. "You know how she likes to get out and go everywhere no matter what kind of weather it is. She forgets she's seventy-one years old."

"Big Momma and Argentina both keep their feet in the road all the time," said Antoine, "going everywhere day and night."

If I hadn't got worried over Big Momma being sick, I might have laughed over what Momma said about checkers. Big Momma and I played at least twenty games a weekend. In a couple of minutes, pine tree tops, then palmetto heads and trunks, and finally, sandy shoreline came into view. We were almost at Cuffy's Island. Thank goodness!

Big Momma lived at the end of a narrow, red dirt road that everybody called Big Momma's Creek Road. It connected with Montegue's Ferry Boat Road.

The stream that wound around her house was called Big Momma's Creek. It had the fattest crabs, the biggest fish, the juiciest shrimp, and the fullest clams and oysters around. Of course, we had a secret for why that was. We threw most of her vegetable and meat scraps in the water. One time I caught a three-pound flounder on a chunk of chicken liver.

After we drove off the ferry, we turned right onto Big Momma's Creek Road, and bumped across the wooden bridge over her creek. In a few minutes we were at her house.

Big Momma opened the door, smiling and pulling her housecoat around her. Bullet banged his tail hard against our legs. "I declare, Bullet told me you all would be here soon," she said. "For the last fifteen minutes he's been sniffing and scratching around the door something fierce."

Momma bustled Big Momma back into the house. "Get back in bed now. You're sick. We'll take care of everything. Move, Bullet. While we do the clothes, we're going to fix enough food to last till I come back for Mary Elouise Sunday afternoon."

Big Momma said humph to that, but she kept smiling. I knew she didn't much care for Momma's cooking. She said Momma didn't add enough salt and pepper to the food, and cooked the vegetables too long.

"And here's my baby," Big Momma said, hugging me. She looked the same. I was relieved about that. "You might as well forget about beating me at checkers this weekend. I'm gonna win 'em all."

"Are you bad sick, Big Momma?" I asked.

"Not so sick," she said. "Your momma just likes to make a fuss."

"I'm gonna be in a play," I told her, "that—"

"That she doesn't want to be in," Momma said. "Here we go again. I told her she wasn't going to stand up there and act stupid like she did in that pageant."

I pressed my lips together and looked down at the floor. I bet she'd never forget what happened in that dumb pageant.

"She's gonna do a good job this time," Big Momma said, patting my cheek. "You just watch and see."

Momma ordered Big Momma to bed. "You know a cold's nothing to play with in the middle of winter at your age. Course, I think you got the flu. Come on now, get in bed!" She went to the refrigerator and looked in it. "Either flu or cold can turn into double pneumonia just like that with you older people. This is the third time this winter you had to be down in the bed."

Big Momma stuck her tongue at her. "I hear you signifying about my age. I can still out-walk you any day, Shenetta."

"And put those big pink fuzzy slippers on your feet when you're out of bed; they're warmer," Momma went on. "I heard a person can get pneumonia through their bare feet."

"Hush up, please! I give, I give! I'm going, I'm going!" Big Momma hurried into bed and propped a pillow against each ear. Bullet dropped his big brown body on the rug by her bed, plopped his huge head on her old brown slippers, and rolled his yellow eyes up at us.

We all laughed, even Momma.

We sorted, washed, dried, folded, and ironed everybody's clothes. Big Momma watched us from her bed. "You got to wash that gold sweater separate," she called out. "And please don't wash my good jeans with the boys' old blue jeans."

Momma pulled Big Momma's jeans back out of the washer. "We know how to do."

When we weren't working with clothes we were in the kitchen cooking greens, pinto beans, meat loaf, mashed potatoes, cornbread, and beef broth. I liked all that, but I wished we could have some hot dogs, chocolate cake, and fried chicken, too.

"Don't put all the ham hocks in the beans," Big Momma hollered. "I like 'em in the greens, too, you know."

"Big Momma, I know how to cook your greens and navy beans," Momma hollered back. "Been doing it for years." But Argentina and I looked at each other. When Momma left the kitchen, Argentina tiptoed to the stove. With a big spoon she lifted some ham hocks from the beans and dropped them into the greens.

I looked out the kitchen window. Andrew and Antoine were having a sword fight with the rake handles. "Let's go to the creek," I heard Andrew say.

"Not yet," Antoine said back. "Bam! Got ya!"

Argentina bumped me out of her way with her hip. "Quick, set the table for me. I got to zip. Carlotta's waiting for me down at the Unity Club."

I knew she and Carlotta wanted to meet some boys. The Unity Club was the boarded-up brown brick community center building about a mile up the road from Big Momma's. Kids stood around outside, fooled around, and listened to music on their boom boxes. Older guys washed their cars. The Unity Club sat by the Eureka Hall Masonic Lodge and the Kings of the Coastal Plains No. 6 Elks Lounge. Pops Pazant's Grocery Store was on the other side. If I didn't have so much to talk about to Big Momma—and if I didn't have to set the table—I'd have wanted to go there myself.

But before Argentina could get her foot out of the door, Momma called her back in. "Where do you think you're going? It's dark outside. It's time to eat, and I told you not to go anywhere, anyway. Don't even try it."

"Shoot!" Argentina stuck out her lip.

Momma let Big Momma out of bed long enough to eat. "The only way you're gonna get better is to rest and take your medicine," Momma reminded her. "You should have pulled out of this sickness long before now. And stay out of that garden."

"This is just a touch of arthritis," Big Momma said. "I know I didn't need to be hoeing in the garden with the ground still so wet. But I'll be fine. You talk like I got one foot in the grave, Shenetta."

"Mary Elouise, you make sure she stays in

bed all weekend, you hear?" Momma told me. "Make sure she eats every drop of that beef broth and takes her medicine. Big Momma, don't take so much mashed potatoes! You're overweight now!"

"Hush up and let me eat in peace," Big Momma laughed. "Mary Elouise, ask your momma how I'm supposed to drink up all that broth and not eat anything to keep it from swishing around in my stomach." But she lifted a tablespoon of mashed potatoes off her plate and put it on Antoine's plate. "There. And that's okay about me being overweight. If I want to be fat now that I'm seventy-one years old, I will. Antoine, your momma is worse than Dr. Galbreath, always trying to stuff folks full of poison and put them to bed."

She stood up from the table, then patted Momma's hand. "I'm just funnin', Shenetta, you're the Lord's blessing to me, though, you truly are. You've always been there when I needed you. Oh, I got a fine family. Two fine young grandsons, these fine two granddaughters here. I'll be all right with Mary Elouise with me. She's always such a big help. Now you go on back home, and we'll see you Sunday morning. I want to go to church."

Everybody said their good-byes to us, and Momma helped Big Momma into bed.

As soon as they had left the house and the car had pulled out of the driveway, Big Momma slid out of bed. "C'mon, Mary Elouise, let's play." She picked up the checkerboard set and the sack of checkers and, limping over to her favorite chair, set the board on the cocktail table in front of it. I flopped down by the table, on the shag rug.

Big Momma sipped on her diet Seven Up, and I sipped on my strawberry Koolaid. We were ready. "Set up that board!" she laughed. "I'm gonna beat you up one wall and down the other."

"I'm ahead. I wrote it down." I pulled my little notebook out of the sack and turned to last week's scores. "I beat you fifteen games; you only beat me eleven. So I'm the champ!"

"Oh really? Mighty big words there, bub."

After she won two games and I won three, I figured it was time to talk. "Big Momma, there's this girl at school. And she wants to be friends with this other girl. But no matter what this girl does to be nice to her, this other girl won't be nice back. This girl is nice to some other girl."

"So?"

"What should she do? The girl who wants to be friends with this girl, I mean."

"Whew, slow down now," Big Momma said. "Don't get me confused." She thought for a minute. "Well, that's hard to say. It's good to have friends. You don't need a whole lot. You won't get a whole lot, anyway. Nobody does."

She studied the checkerboard. "You can't be friends with some people, no matter how hard you try. They won't let you. So you just be friendly when they do let you. If they don't, you just tip your hat, say hello, and keep on trucking. You don't need to run after folks and beg for their friendship."

Did that mean I didn't have a chance to be Brandy's best friend? Ever? That sounded awful. Depressed, I tried to concentrate on the game. Big Momma won again. "But what if this girl is so sharp, and she does everything you ever want to do?" I said. "What if she's got fine clothes, and long blonde hair, and she's rich? If she and this other girl could be best friends, they could go everywhere, and they'd be the most popular kids in school."

"Crown me, please," said Big Momma.

I dropped a checker on top of the one of Big Momma's that had reached my king's row. "See, Big Momma, there's this girl at school and her name is Brandy. And I'm the one who's trying to be her friend. This is for real." I told her everything I'd done to be Brandy's friend. I told her about Kenyatta, too. "But you just said I gotta give up on Brandy."

Big Momma patted her foot. "Well, Namesake, if you can love yourself for who you are without going overboard about it, your friends'll come natural. And don't forget your old friends, like Hattie, while you're chasing after this new one."

She told me not to be so hard on myself. "You can do anything you want to do within reason if you put your mind to it—good or bad. You just have to remember to do good, which is harder to do. You might get this child to be your friend, or you might not." She gave me a big smile. "You'll know what to do. You're such a smart little lady."

I thought that over, then something hit me. "But Momma says I'm stupid." Tears jumped into my eyes. "She said I was an ugly ole Black thing when I told her about . . . about— And I got in trouble at school 'cause Miz Thomas said I had an attitude problem, and then this storyteller lady caught me when I was in Mr. Kwanzaa's bag trying to take back my—"

"Oh, Namesake, you been put through the wringer, haven't you? Come here." She patted her big, soft lap, and I climbed right into it. I told her about Miz Vereen, the name-calling between Hattie and Libby, Dr. King's birthday, my part, the book, and the whole business about the story. I didn't tell her about the dolls, though.

Big Momma said "my goodness" and "poor baby" all the way through. When I finally finished, she poked out her lips and hummed. "Your momma didn't mean to talk bad about your color, honey. She didn't mean it the way it came out, 'cause you're her child, and the Lord meant for you to be the color you are. Mary Elouise, we should never talk nasty about somebody's skin color, starting with our own race. Your momma was wrong to do that to you."

She said Miz Vereen grew up believing the wrong things about our people. "She doesn't know any different. She does need to learn the truth, though. I bet your other teachers are trying to show her the right way to do. Boy, have they got a job!" She let out a big laugh. "She doesn't mean any harm, even though it sounds like she's doing some. You say she likes you? That's good. You keep on liking her, too, honey. She'll straighten up one day soon. She better. Otherwise *I'll* have to come talk to her, too."

She shook her head. "This business about Black folks' hair and skin color has had our race confused for years and years. A long time ago a gal called me 'baldie' and I almost popped her upside her head with my umbrella. She was jealous 'cause my hair looked nice and hers didn't. We had both just come out of the beauty parlor, too, and we had the same length of hair. But then I realized that she was just ignorant. Hattie and Libby were ignorant for calling names, too. So are grown folks when they do it."

Big Momma said one time she had stepped out of church and was dressed sharp in new clothes from top to bottom. "And durned if I didn't hear this chick say, 'humph, look at that ugly ole Black

✳ 155 ✳

Mary Elouise in that ole raggedy dress.' Said it on church grounds, too!" Big Momma shook her head. "You might hear Rev. Walker preach about who Black people's enemies are in this world, but sometimes we are our own worst enemy. Some of us still have to learn to treat each other better."

I hadn't thought about it that way, but she was right. I was my own worst enemy when it came to that story. Big Momma leaned over with me still in her lap, and jumped over two of my men.

"Hey!" I scrambled out of her lap to my side of the board. But then I was able to jump three of hers. "I win!" I stuck out my chest.

"Sure did! Good for you. That's enough checkers for now. Mary Elouise, this business about this girl Brandy has got to sit in my mind a while. But don't worry, everything will be all right. You'll see."

She got into bed, and told me to put Bullet out for a while. I did, then crawled into bed in front of her, snuggled myself in close, and glued my eyes to the TV. It was toasty warm in bed with Big Momma, and all my problems seemed far away.

CHAPTER

TEN

"Big Momma, are you awake?"

I sat up in bed and patted her on the arm. It was Saturday morning, almost 9:30.

Big Momma opened one eye, then the other, and yawned. "I'll be moving directly, baby. My old friend Mr. Arthur Itis is visiting again."

"You want some aspirin for ole Arthur Itis?" I knew she meant her arthritis was bothering her. She kept her medicine in a drawer of her night stand right by the bed.

I set the bottle on top of the stand, and brought her a fresh glass of water from the bathroom. Her eyeglasses were close by. So were her false teeth. She called them her choppers. They sat in another glass of water grinning back at me.

Big Momma slowly sat up. She sighed and swung her legs out of bed. When she saw me watching her, she stood up. "Fly away, ole pain and sorrow, I got to get on out this bed," she sang. "Shoot, we got things to do. We need to go down to Pops's store and look over his cabbage sprouts. I'd like to set some out when the weather warms up a tad bit more."

"But Momma said you had to stay in bed."

"I know what I want to do. At my age, I'd dry out and turn to dust lying in bed all day. Where's my choppers? Let's get to gettin'."

We flew around fixing breakfast. Well, I did. Big Momma still moved slowly. She rubbed her knees and said, "Oh my." She let me fix some grits and toast.

After breakfast I threw on my clothes. Then I sat tapping my foot, waiting on Big Momma. She pulled on a pair of blue jeans and her Benedict College sweatshirt, a pair of green wooly socks, some tennis shoes, and her heavy blue jacket. She wrapped a thick scarf around her neck, too. Big Momma said she was cold-blooded, and all winter dressed like it was a hundred below zero outside. Inside the house, she kept the heat on high so she could wear just her housecoat and her old brown slippers without worrying.

"You sure you're all right?" I asked. She nodded. "When's Mr. Montegue gonna plow up the garden?"

"He can't. His tractor broke down." She pulled on her knit cap and her gloves. "His brother Ed's coming out with his tiller maybe next week or so. I wonder if Pops has any onions. They like this cool weather."

"Yuk! You oughta grow some chocolate cake and hot dogs!"

We headed out for Mr. Pazant's Grocery Store. It was chilly outside, but not real cold. The sun was shining, too. Bullet trotted ahead of us in the road, which ran close to the creek. I could see two white herons stalking through the green swamp grass near the opposite creek bank, looking in the water for mud minnows. Bullet lunged at the birds from our side and barked hard. They ignored him.

"You know, I been thinking on what you told me last night about that girl," Big Momma said.

"You mean Brandy?"

"That's the one. She sounds nice enough. I just wonder, though, if it's worth you going through all this headache over her."

I started to feel helpless. "But what else can I do, Big Momma?"

"There might not be anything left for you to do is what I'm saying. Some folks just don't have enough in common to be friends."

"But we're both in the play and we both got mouse pins and we're both in fourth grade—"

"You and a bunch of other girls, I bet."

She's telling you to give up, said Mary Inside. I sure didn't want to do that! We walked on.

After a while Big Momma spoke. "Your part in the play sounds hard, I'll say that. But if you go to work on it and get it in shape, you'll be tops. You can do it."

She must have seen me frown, because she added, "Though you don't think so, do you?"

I kicked rocks in the road. "Not really."

Big Momma stopped me in the middle of the road. She hooked her cane over her right arm, and pressed both hands on my shoulders. "Mary Elouise Avery, you gotta start thinking about what you *can* do, not what you *can't!* You wanted to be in the play, and now you are! Good for you! Don't you know that if you keep your face down in the mud, all you're gonna learn about is dirt? But if you pull your head out from that hole in the ground and look up, you'll see all kinds of things to find out about."

She went on like that for a while. Yeah, yeah, tell me anything, said Mary Inside. I'm dumb.

"And stop rolling your eyes at me," she said firmly, "or I'll bop that little hardhead side of you right in the chops." She grabbed her cane and pounded it on the ground as she talked.

Mary Inside shut up.

Big Momma kept on talking and pounding until she made me promise that I'd do my very best with that ole part.

"Let's make a deal." She stuck out her hand. "You be tops in learning that part, and I promise I'll come to your play, no matter what. Deal?"

"Deal! Oh goody!" I jumped up and down, and shook her hand hard, glad that she'd be there. She hadn't been able to come to the pageant last year because she'd been sick.

"Don't be surprised if I still don't get this stuff right," I told her. "Brandy's memorized hers already. So's Kenyatta. I'll never be as good as Brandy."

"Mary Elouise, don't you EVER say some such again! You're equal to anybody else in being able to do. You're just as good, you hear?" She put her right arm around my shoulders, and we walked along. "Have I ever lied to you? Look me in the eye and say I have. Have I?"

"No, m'am."

"I'm not about to now. Listen to me, honey. You and Brandy aren't on the same wavelink, at least not yet. But it sounds like this other girl and you are."

"Kenyatta?" I shook my head. I still remembered the story I'd written about her. I don't think she ever found out. She was all right, I guess. But she wasn't Brandy.

"We all got to learn to be our own best friends first, Mary Elouise, and do what we can to work on being good to ourselves. You're just as good as anybody else."

I shook my head. "Not as good as Brandy. She's way better than me. She's smart and got a lot of money, sharp clothes, long blonde hair, blue eyes, just like Barbie on 'Barbie's Adventures.' And—"

"Oh my. I see what your problem is." Big Momma sighed. "You and I got a mighty big job to do. You don't think you're as good as this particular little *white* girl is what it is, isn't it? And you think she's better than you, so you want to be like her. And maybe then other folks will act toward you the way they act toward her. Isn't that it?"

My face got hot. "Oh, unh, I didn't mean better! I meant, see, unh—"

"Baby, nobody's better than you, 'cause you're my grandchild, and I'm proud of you. Are you gonna tell me I'm wrong?"

She gave me her long, soft look. I shook my head.

"Open your mouth. Am I wrong?" She said it louder, and tickled me on the neck with her fingers. "Hunh?"

"No," I said, giggling now.

"Then you say it out loud so I'll know for sure." Big Momma put both hands on her hips. Her cane dangled from her wrist. "Say 'I'm pretty and I am the best there is 'cause Big Momma said so.' "

I shook my head. I could see Pops's store, and his grandkids Ron and Sequoia outside it, looking our way. I started to giggle. They'd think I was crazy, screaming and shouting.

"Say it now. Don't waste time. We got to get on to the store."

I shook my head. "I can't. People will hear."

"Well, let 'em hear. I want 'em to hear. Say it, or I'll sit right down here in the cold dirt and not budge till you do. Cars can come by and run me over so many times I'll look like one of those dead possums smashed flat on the road with their tail straight out. I'll stay here right smack dab plastered to the road till you talk."

"Big Momma!" I didn't want her to end up like that! Plus, we'd have to be here all day waiting for a car.

When Big Momma started to squat, I took a deep breath. "I'm—I'm—what'd you say?"

"I'm pretty and I'm the best there is 'cause Big Momma said so."

"I'm pretty—"

"Louder!"

I saw Ron and Sequoia wave at us. "—And I'm the best—"

"Louder!"

"—And I'm the best there is—"

"Holler, dag-gum it!"

"—The best there is 'cause Big Momma said so!" I screamed.

"Thank you. Now we can get on to Pops's."

I felt weird inside hollering about being pretty, but it was a good weird, kind of like how I felt when Miz Imani said so. We walked up Pops's sawdust path.

"Howdy," said Pops to Big Momma.

"Hey," said Ron and Sequoia to me. I liked Ron and Sequoia. They lived on Cuffy's Island, but went to my school. They rode a boat to school every day. Sequoia was in third grade and Ron was in fifth.

We said howdy and hey back and followed Pops into the shop. Bullet flopped down in the sawdust by the door.

I liked being in Pops's store. It was crammed to the ceiling with practically everything. Square blue-and-black car batteries were on the floor. Water hoses and used tires hung from the rafters and were piled up against the back wall. Cans of chicken noodle soup, spaghetti, and sliced peaches, sacks of white cornmeal, flour, sugar, and coffee clustered together on the shelves. Wooden clothes baskets of yams and white potatoes sat on the floor. Plastic baskets with sewing thread, bars of soap, light bulbs, socks, white plastic forks, toothpaste, and Wiffle balls sat in a row in the middle of the store.

A refrigerator with soda pop, and another refrigerator with beer and wine sat by the front counter. Potato chips hung on racks. Bubble gum and candy bars were piled in boxes on the front counter by a huge jar of ugly pinkish-red pickled pigs' feet.

Toilet paper, detergent, bleach, glue, and pencils lay in baskets in front of the counter on the floor. Bullets and BBs were in a locked glass shelf behind the counter. I could wander around in there all day and not see everything.

"What were you guys hollering about back there in the road?" Ron asked.

My face got hot. "Nothing."

"I heard it," said Sequoia. "You were talking about 'Big Momma something something.' "

We followed Big Momma and Pops to a shed behind the store. Pops kept his plants on rows of benches in a little damp, sunny room there. Pops called this his greenhouse. It smelled like dirt, horse manure, and sawdust.

He pointed to boxes of small, green-gray plants with fat, oval shaped leaves. "These cabbages will be ready to set out in about ten days. Onions you can set out now if your ground is ready."

"Which it's not, so I might have to hold off on them," Big Momma said. "I'll call Ed soon's we get back home. Maybe he can speed up his plans to turn over my ground. And I gotta do something with my peach trees. Last year they had just little bitty, wormy peaches. They did so poorly that the kids didn't even sneak around and steal them off the trees. That was the only good thing came out of it. Parents don't teach their children anymore how to respect other people's property."

She smiled when she said that, but I knew who she meant. Ron was awful about stealing Big Momma's peaches. He even broke some branches one year.

"Prune those peach trees," said Pops. "Then take a rusty nail and pound it into the base of each tree trunk. I guarantee you'll have big, juicy fruit this summer." He looked at Ron. "And let me know if anybody comes sneaking around stealing. I'll tan their hides good."

Ron, Sequoia, and I headed back to the counter up front.

"Told you you'd get in trouble about her peaches," said Sequoia.

He shrugged and grinned. He was sandy-haired and light-skinned, with freckles. "Mary Elouise, how about one of these delicious pickled pigs' feetses?"

He pointed to the large glass jar half-filled with oily brown water. In the water were eight or nine pigs' hooves still attached to the ankles. They looked like fat pink hairless puppy paws to me. Yuck! They smelled like sour pickles. I touched one once. It felt like greasy cold leather. It had a sticky sound to it when I rubbed my finger over it. I tasted one once, too. It tasted like how rotten fish smell.

Ron pretended to open the jar and bite into a pigsfoot. Sequoia and I stuck our fingers in our mouths like we wanted to throw up.

"And in the middle of the night, when the moon is full, the feetses come out this jar," said Ron in a low, ghostly voice.

"How're they gonna get out?" Sequoia asked.

"They unscrew the lid with their feetses," he told her. "And the feetses crawl down this jar to the counter." His fingers hip hopped down the jar. "They gallop down Big Momma's Creek Road." His fingers tripped across the counter toward my hand, which I moved. "Then the feetses bust down the door and get ya! Oink! Oink!" Wiggling all ten fingers in my face, he jumped at me.

I screamed. "Better stop! You're NOT funny!"

One time I told Ron about this nightmare I had. I dreamed that pigsfeet creatures from outer space got into my bed, and chased me out of my house. They chased me down the street and into my school. They got so close that I could hear them breathing hard and grinding their teeth. Then I woke up, and praise the Lord I was still alive. The pigsfeet didn't get me. Ron tried to, though, every chance he got.

When Big Momma and I got back home, she

decided to take a rest and to watch TV, which was fine with me. Wrestling was on. In the first match this big fat guy with a red Z painted on his chest and a thick, long, brown and yellow braid dangling down his back hissed into the announcer's microphone. His name was Z Rattler. Sometimes he had wire hidden in that braid and used it to choke people. Sometimes he had pieces of steel hidden in it and whacked people in the head with it. When he got mad he'd grab his braid and shake it like it was a rattlesnake's tail. When his opponents got mad, they'd grab that braid and shake old Rattler, just like he was a rattlesnake's tail, too. They'd drag him around the ring by that braid. He'd be screeching and hissing.

"That fella is a pistol, isn't he?" said Big Momma. "Carrying on about what all he's gonna do to everybody, and can't do a thing!" She slurped her coffee, then leaned toward me. "Lemme hear you talk out your part while we're watching this foolish commercial."

"Aw, do I have to now?"

"When else are you gonna do it?"

"Later." I stared at the TV. Z Rattler's opponent this time was a guy wearing a Lone Ranger mask and a construction hat. He had muscles all over the place. His name was Hi Ho Hard Hat Hercules.

"Don't put off till later what you can get started on now."

I dragged my bag over and pulled out my part. "Africans first came to American shores as slaves in 1619," I began.

"Whoa, that's not right," said Big Momma. "Some of us got here before 1619 and not as slaves, either. I read somewhere that some Africans had their own ships and sailed to the New World long before Columbus was even thought of. Oh well, go ahead, read on."

I paused. "I never heard that before."

"Go ahead, read on."

"These im-im-impoverished Black Americans made unh, unh, what does s-i-g-n-i-f-i-c-a-n-t spell?"

"Significant."

"—Made significant gains after they were freed by President Lincoln when in 1863 he signed the E-m-a-n-c-i-p-a—"

"Emancipation Proclamation. That part's not quite right, either." Big Momma was frowned up. "His signing it didn't automatically make us free. How would we have known about it? No TV or radio back then, and we weren't allowed to read, you know. That thing took years, baby! Remember, too, that some of us were free way before then. We did all kinds of significant things without having to be slaves! We weren't all impoverished, either. Impoverished? That means poor, honey. Course now, you got to hand it to those ole slaves. They did a whole, whole lot of things people don't give em credit for. Like building this country."

She pecked me on the knee. "But child, we had a long, long history in Africa first. Africa had kings and queens and universities when Europe and England and America were still winks in the good Lord's eye."

"I know about a queen named Nefer-something." I grabbed the book Miz Imani had given to us, and flipped through the pages until I found the queen's picture. I showed it to Big Momma.

"Nefertiti, African queen from Egypt. Now, honey, there was some true royalty for you." Big Momma thumbed through the book. When I told her who I got it from, she got real interested in Miz Imani, too.

"It was surely nice of her to give you this. Born right on Turner's Isle, you say. I bet there's truth in her book about our people that you won't find much anywhere else. Take that Harriet Tubman." She found Harriet Tubman's picture in the book. "Now there was another top lady for you. She was a queen, too, in her own way."

Big Momma read me the story of Harriet Tubman, stopping now and then to add information not in the book. She told me how Harriet Tubman led a bunch of Union boats down the Combahee River in South Carolina near Beaufort during the Civil War in 1863 and saved 700 people from slavery. I was impressed. I hadn't heard *that* before, either.

"So you don't need to ever be ashamed 'cause some of our kin were slaves. There was a whole, whole lot more to us than what we did to keep the master happy. You better try to make the master happy! You might get beat to pieces if you didn't. That part was just plain common sense. Don't ever kick an alligator barefoot, in other words!"

She let out a great shout of laughter, and laughed until she had to cough. "People all over the world were slaves at one time or another. A lot of the white people who came to this country were criminals, too, kicked out of England." She laughed again. "Bet you didn't know that, did you? But it all worked out. We're all in this together. None of one's better than the other, past or present, I always say."

She shook her finger at me, wound up now. "Shoot, our ancestors didn't jump in line over in Africa to sign up to be slaves for over here like they were looking for jobs. No! They had their own homes and families. But some evil Europeans and some evil Americans and some evil English and some evil Africans got together and put the finger on other Africans."

She said that those old Africans who ended up slaves did everything they could to keep their families together here as best they could, even though so many got sold apart and never seen again.

I wanted to ask her if she knew any old Africans. I was afraid, though, that she might think I meant was *she* that old.

"But we're not kin to Africans anymore, are we, Big Momma?"

She frowned at me. "Of course we're kin! Where do you think you came from? Off a pine tree?"

"But nobody in our family runs around naked with bones in their noses, with their hair looking like Buckwheat, saying booga booga."

"Child, what in the good Lord's name are you talking about?" She put her hand on my forehead. "Are you sick? You got a fever? Or just been watching too many of those stupid Tarzan movies? Buckwheat! Bone in the nose! Naked! Lord Jesus, what do they teach you children in school these days? Don't know where you're going and don't know where you been—white, Black, yellow, red, or brown. No wonder you're running in circles."

She said humph, humph, humph for a while.

"How many times have I told you about your great-great-grandmam Lela? She was straight

* 172 *

from Africa. Had tribal scars on her face. Don't screw up your nose. Those were beauty marks. Lela wasn't her real African name, and I can't think of it right now, but it'll come to me. She was way up in age when she passed. I was ten years old. I loved that poor ole soul with all my heart."

"I remember you saying something about great-great-grandmam Lela," I said, "but I didn't know she was from Africa."

"You shoulda figured it out."

"Did she have a bone in her nose and not wear any clothes?" This was important to me.

"No, Mary Elouise Avery, she did not have a bone in her nose." Frowning, Big Momma rapidly blinked her eyes at me with each word. "And she wore clothes. But if she did have a bone in her nose, so what? When you wear my hair combs, you got bones in your hair. You got pieces of wire in your ears right now."

I fingered the earrings in my pierced ears. Earrings were different. Weren't they?

Big Momma smiled. She stopped blinking. She took off her glasses, and leaned her forehead against mine. "But it's all right for you to ask questions, Namesake. That's what you're supposed to do. If you don't ask, you won't know. Your questions make me remember, so I can pass everything on to you."

I snuggled up against her shoulder. "Tell me some more about Great-Great-Grandmam Lela. And talk about Daddy."

"Okay. And then we'll get back to your part in that play. I wouldn't mind touching it up just a little, change some of those words. Maybe that'll help make it easier for you to say your piece. You tell Miz Thomas *I* did it. Whoever wrote your part must have been reading *Gone With the Wind* at the same time."

I just snuggled. How could Big Momma know so much about how I thought? After all the stuff she told me tonight, and what Miz Imani said, maybe being Black wasn't so bad after all.

Suddenly I sat up and pointed to the TV. "Look! Hi Ho Hard Hat Hercules has ole Rattler by the braid! Listen to him hiss!"

CHAPTER

ELEVEN

Back at school Monday it was hard for me to not jump up first to be by Brandy in the lines for recess and lunch. I could have got right by her three times. But I was gonna follow Big Momma's advice, and leave her alone. It sure wasn't easy, though.

I tried not to even look at her and Kenyatta and Yolanda in the cafeteria during play rehearsal. Instead, I sat by myself and studied my lines, just like Big Momma had told me to. When my turn came, I didn't do as bad as I'd done before, either. I only made about half a dozen mistakes.

Kenyatta came over to me. "You sounded good on your part."

I looked away, surprised and pleased by her compliment. "But I can't get it all memorized."

"I can tell you how I do it," she said. "You want some help?"

"Naw, I can do it." I put my papers up to my face so she couldn't see me. I don't know why. Mary Inside must have put me up to it.

Kenyatta stood up. "Well, good luck."

I felt bad that I acted so mean to her. I wished I could let myself like her as much as I liked Brandy. I promised myself that I'd be nicer to her, too, since she insisted on being so nice to me. And I tried not to think about Brandy.

By Wednesday Hattie had noticed and approved of my new change over Brandy.

"Came back to the real world, hunh?" she said to me as I walked home with her and Maizell.

I told her what Big Momma had said. "Well, I'm sure glad to hear that." Hattie grinned wider than I'd seen her do in a long time. "You know, people were starting to talk about you and call you names, especially Libby Burns. Listen, Timika, Alicia, and I've been studying our parts over at the rec center. We're gonna meet again Thursday after school. Wanna join us?"

I felt hurt. "How come you haven't said anything to me before now?"

"Don't jump bad with me. You're the one didn't want your part. I like mine. This is the first time I'm in something other than the back row of chorus. Plus, you had Brandy-itis."

"Not anymore." Well, not as much, I told myself.

"Are you guys fighting again?" asked Maizell. When we both said no, she looked relieved.

We walked past the Gumbo Grove Recreation Center. It was right by our school. It was a long, yellow and blue brick building with an indoor swimming pool, a gymnasium, and indoor and outdoor tennis courts. One time I took a cheerleading class over there, but I dropped out after the second lesson.

"By the way," Hattie said, looking at me out of the side of her eye, "Kenyatta's coming, too."

When I frowned, Hattie told me to quit acting dumb. "What's Kenyatta ever done mean to you? I don't know why you don't like her. Everybody else does. She's not stuck up or sometimey like Brandy is. When people cracked on you chasing after Brandy, I was embarrassed because I had to stand there and take it."

"You shoulda said something."

Hattie folded her arms. "Like what?"

I couldn't think of anything. "*Everybody* was talking?"

"Everybody in fourth grade at least." Hattie ticked off people on her fingers. "Him and him and her and her and her, and she did, and she did, too."

"That's not everybody."

"Close enough."

"Well, I'm not chasing anybody anymore." I hadn't heard a word folks had been saying. Now I felt really embarrassed. I told Hattie I'd practice with them. We said our good-byes and promised to call each other later.

When I saw Pooch and Jamal walking home behind me, I wondered if they'd been laughing, too. And what about Chaundra? I remembered how she screamed over what Libby had called Hattie. There were Yolanda and Timika on the other side of the street. Were they laughing, too? I hurried home, wanting to get out of sight from everybody.

As soon as I turned on "Barbie's Adventures" at home the telephone rang. It was Big Momma. "Hope you had a good day today," she said.

When I told her that I did, she said good. "I knew you could do it if you put your mind to it. Now go over your part, right from the start."

I asked her to wait a minute while I got it. When I hurried past the TV set, there was that new girl, Keisha, dancing her eyes out on a new song. She was good, too. That song was so sharp I had to tap my foot. I bet I could lip sync that. Oops! Big Momma! I flew back to the hallway.

"How're you feeling, Big Momma?"

"Oh, fair, fair. I got to go to the doctor this

✳ 178 ✳

Friday for a checkup. I'll let you know what time your momma can bring you out to the house."

"You're still coming to the play, aren't you?"

"Nothing can stop me from seeing my baby do her thing this time, the Lord willing, of course."

Thursday after school Hattie, Alicia, and I ran over to the rec center. Kids had already filled up part of the lobby, waiting to get into the gym and the swimming pool. Book bags, back packs, note-books, shoes, lunch buckets, and towels were piled every which way on the floor. Everybody talked and laughed at once.

I saw Jermaine and Pooch walk into the Ping-Pong room and jump into crowds of boys grabbing for paddles on the tables.

"Where're we gonna practice?" I asked.

"That corner's our usual spot," said Hattie. "Quick, let's get it!" We scrambled over to the beanbag-chair corner. It was a good place because you could see outside and also see the TV set in the supervisor's office.

As I got myself settled down in the beanbag chair, I saw Kenyatta and Timika bounce through the doors over to us. Kenyatta gave me a real friendly smile. I remembered to smile back.

Hattie took charge, of course. "The choral rappers get to practice first," she said. "C'mon, Timika, give them your paper so they can check what we say. You and me can read off mine."

When Timika handed the sheet to me, Alicia and Kenyatta scooted their bags closer to mine so they could see. "I still can't see," said Alicia. She squeezed in by me on my bag, and Kenyatta squeezed in on the other side. I kept it to myself, but I felt popular all of a sudden.

"Okay, one, two, three! Start!" Hattie ordered. But Timika wasn't ready. She pulled off her glasses to clean them. Timika had an elaborate cleaning process, with special paper and special liquid that came in a little squeeze bottle. She squeezed a drop of liquid on each lens, one drop at a time. Stuff dropped like thick syrup. We waited for the drops to drop. Then she had to scrub each lens with little pieces of paper. Then she had to look for streaks. She held her glasses up at the ceiling and studied them. We crowded together to look up through her glasses, too. Looked clear enough to me. But I wondered how Timika could see streaks without her glasses on.

"Timika! You guys! Hey, c'mon!" yelled Hattie. "Timika! Okay, okay, you ready now? Timika, you ready? You ready? Hunh? Okay, one, two, three, start!"

We're Here to Say
That on This Day
A Mighty Man Was Born

was the first stanza.

So Honesty
We Sell a Braid!
Evybody Com Bow Ya Hone!

was what they said for the second one.

"What?" we all said. "Hunh?"

Hattie got mad. "You'all don't know diddly squat! Alicia's deaf, Mary Elouise can't hear, and Kenyatta wasn't listening!"

"I heard every word, and wasn't a single one you said that's in the second stanza," said Alicia. "You flew through it like birds after bugs."

Timika got mixed up the next time. We made them say that second stanza of the rap five more times until we agreed they had it right. This was fun!

When Kenyatta said her speech I finally knew now who she was playing—Sojourner Truth. I'd seen that name in the book Miz Imani gave me. It called Sojourner Truth an African queen from America. Dr. King was in there, too. Kenyatta put a lot of feeling in her voice when she spoke. I followed every word on her paper. She got every word right. It was beautiful, I had to admit. We clapped when she was through.

"How can you memorize everything so easy?" I finally had to ask. Monday I hadn't wanted to find out. I sure did now.

"I'm just lucky," was all she said.

"Geez, what a brain," said Hattie. "You must just read it one or two times, then stamp everything in your brain. They call that having a photo-something."

Kenyatta smiled, and her dimples stood out, but she still didn't say anything.

"Stop, you guys, you're embarrassing her," said Timika.

Jermaine, Jamal, and Pooch ran out of the Ping-Pong room to us. "What're you guys doin' now?" Pooch said. They bent over us, panting.

"Go way," said Hattie. "We're working on our play parts again. No boys. Bye."

We all jerked our thumbs at them to leave, trying not to giggle at how stupid they looked hanging over us.

Pooch kept staring at Kenyatta, but she wouldn't look at him. He kicked her beanbag a couple times. She still didn't say anything. Suddenly she looked up and smiled at him. His face lit up like a street lamp.

Hattie and Timika loudly began chanting their rap song again.

When I asked Jermaine how he was doing with his speech, he shook his head and looked sad. "I can get through most of it, but I can't seem to remember enough of it or pronounce the words so that they make sense. Sure glad I don't have to give the whole speech."

He looked so sad that I felt sorry for him. "Can't you and Pooch practice?"

"He says going in to Miz Thomas every day for help is enough for him."

Kenyatta heard Jermaine. "Maybe Miz Thomas could help you, too."

"Yeah," he said. I could tell, though, that he didn't want to do that.

"Maybe you can get in our group, Jermaine," Kenyatta said.

Jermaine perked up for a moment. "Can I?"

"Nope, nope, nope," Hattie said. "You guys'll just mess things up, and we'd never get anything done!"

"C'mon, Pooch." Jermaine grabbed hold of Pooch by the jacket sleeve. "I don't want to be around a bunch of stupid girls, anyhow." He stamped away.

"Maybe we should have let him in," said Kenyatta.

"If he comes through again, we'll vote on it," Hattie said. "Now, back to business."

The next day when I saw Jermaine he wanted to know how our practice went. I told him what we'd decided. "I can't sit up in the middle of a bunch of girls," he said again, "especially not with Hattie there. She likes to boss too much."

I asked Hattie on the way home how come she didn't want boys in our practice group.

"I don't care if Jermaine joins our group, but I don't want Pooch in."

"Why?"

"Pooch popped in the last time and acted like a fool. He's in love with Kenyatta, you know."

My mouth fell open. "No, I didn't know!"

"That's 'cause you haven't been paying attention to anything. Jermaine's okay. Course, he's not Big Head Thomas you're talking about, or Junebug."

Big Head Thomas and Junebug Hill were fine, fine. They were on the Gumbo Grove Middle School football team. Big Head was the quarterback. I know he liked Raisin.

When I got home, I went straight to my bed and did my homework, then called Big Momma. We worked on my part together. I didn't even turn on the TV.

When Friday came and Momma brought me home from school, I flew around packing stuff to go to Big Momma's. I wanted to stand up in front of her and say my whole part without a single mistake. I knew she'd be so proud. I wanted to try to memorize it this weekend, too.

"What time are we going out to Big Momma's?" I asked Momma. It was already after four o'clock.

Momma hesitated. "Oh, unh, we'll just have to wait till she calls."

Just then the telephone rang. Momma answered it. "Big Momma said to tell you not to come out this weekend," she said after hanging up the phone.

"Why?"

" 'Cause, well, 'cause you can't."

"But why?"

" 'Cause she's in the hospital."

"In the hospital? What's the matter?" I jumped up. "Is she gonna die?" I started to cry.

I never knew Big Momma to be in a hospital before. Would the doctors cut off her leg like they did with Miz Prieleu? She had diabetes, too.

Momma took my wet face between her hands and rubbed away some of my tears. "Oh, she's gonna be all right. Stop that stuff. She's just in for some tests."

"What kind of tests? Is she gonna die?"

"No baby, no, no, she's not gonna die. She's just in for tests, I said."

Momma let me cry against her shoulder for a couple of minutes, then she told me to stop, but I didn't. She told me again, then she shook me a little.

"I said stop now!" Her voice got sharp. "Her sugar's up a little. It's happened before. Maybe you forgot. She hasn't had to go to the hospital lately." Her voice got soft. "Look, honey, we've been knowing for some time that she'd have to go in. It was just a matter of when. They'll probably let her out Monday."

I wished somebody had told me she'd have to go in. I held my breath to try to settle myself down.

Momma said Big Momma would call back to talk to me later on. I cemented myself by the telephone for Big Momma to call. I felt numb all over, like I'd been out in awful cold with no coat on for hours and hours.

Argentina came by. "Gimme the phone. I got to make some calls, okay?"

"Big Momma's gonna call," I said.

"Well, they'll just take a minute. C'mon now. I got some important people waiting to hear my voice."

I warmed up when she said that. I knew about Argentina and her one-minute phone calls. I gathered up my courage. "You better not touch this phone till after Big Momma calls," I said, and set my jaw.

"Well, excuse me!" She frowned, then stopped. "Oh well, you're right," she said. "Be sure to let me talk when she calls, okay?" She went back into our room.

I didn't even move when Momma called us for supper. She brought my plate to me, but I still couldn't eat.

I waited and tried not to think. But I could see Big Momma in my mind. Tubes and needles were stuck every which way in her body. Doctors in white masks with big knives stood all around her. The picture scared me. I tried to hold in my crying, but I couldn't. I cried quiet.

Around eight o'clock Big Momma called. I started to cry again.

"When you coming home from the hospital?"

"How'd you know where I was? Your momma told you, didn't she? Oh, my goodness! I told your Momma I'd tell you where I was. I knew you'd get so much more upset than the others, and I didn't want you to be."

"Are they gonna cut off your leg like they did Miz Prieleu's?"

"Oh no, nothing like that. I'm fine, really I am. Just these ole silly tests. Don't cry, Namesake."

She sure didn't sound like herself, and I said so. "You got your choppers out?"

She told me she'd taken some medicine, and that it had made her sleepy. But I still wasn't satisfied. "I wanna come see you."

"I know," Big Momma said. "Poor little thing. You're so worried about ole Big Momma. Praise God, you're sure my grandbaby."

She waited until I got myself calmed down. Then she made me tell her everything that had happened that day. I told her. She seemed pleased about the practice yesterday, too.

Argentina, Momma, and the boys came in.

"Now I want you to keep on working real hard on that part," Big Momma said. "Try not to get upset about me, you hear? I'll be fine and out of here before you know it. I haven't forgot your program. I'll be there, the Lord willing."

"Okay. Here's everybody." I sure didn't feel like okay, though.

I turned the telephone over to Momma. She talked a little. Then the boys did, and then Argentina did.

"You think we can go see Big Momma in the hospital?" I asked Argentina when she was off the telephone.

"I guess. I heard Momma say she had to run over there tomorrow morning. So we'll probably all go."

CHAPTER

TWELVE

I hardly slept all night, worrying about Big Momma.

Early Saturday morning I slid out of bed and threw my clothes on quick. Argentina and the boys did, too. We were all set to go to the hospital. But Momma said the hospital didn't allow kids under twelve to visit, so we couldn't go.

Our faces frowned up. "That's not fair!"

"Well, I'm thirteen." Argentina reached for her coat.

"I can't take you, either. If I can't take you all, I won't take any. It wouldn't be fair. You understand what I mean, Argentina. Put that lip back in." Momma buttoned up her coat. She opened the front door. "Call Big Momma and tell her I'm running by now to see her before I go to work. I'm off. You all be careful. Argentina? Stay home! Bye."

"Bye!" We rushed to the phone. Argentina got to it first and dialed the hospital for Big Momma, who answered on the second ring to her room. "Hi, Big Momma? Are you all right? Momma said they don't let in kids, so we're calling. And she's on her way. Yes m'am, right now. How're you doin'?"

"Lemme talk!" Antoine grabbed for the phone.

"Stop!" Argentina listened for a few seconds. "And hey, everybody, she says she's fine."

We clapped and hollered. Boy, that took a big load off my mind. "Can I talk next?" I pleaded.

When she held out the phone to me, Antoine grabbed it. "Hey!" I shook his arm, but he wouldn't let go.

"Oh, let him talk," said Argentina, "then you go next."

I sighed hard and frowned, but I just said okay and plopped down on the couch to wait. Of course, when Antoine got through Andrew demanded to go next 'cause he was younger than me. So he did.

"You still there, Big Momma?" was the first thing out of my mouth when I finally got to her.

"Why sure, baby," said Big Momma, "and

been right here all along, in this nice, warm bed, waiting to hear your sweet voice."

"Sure sounds good to hear yours! You coming home today?"

"No, but I'll be home for sure Sunday. I want to go to church Sunday morning, too."

"And about my part in the play? I've been working on it," I told her.

"Good! Let me hear you say it."

I'd just got started good when she told me she'd have to hang up. Her doctor was there.

That gave me a stab of fear. "What's he gonna do to you? Cut off your leg?"

"Hush up. Cut off my leg?" Big Momma laughed. "No, child! But he *is* gonna make sure I get out of this hospital real quick, though, aren't you, Dr. Galbreath? Good morning, doctor. These are my smart grandbabies I'm talking to on the phone."

That made me feel proud. I told her we'd call her back later. I said good-bye.

"We'll wait three hours," said Argentina, "and then call her back."

We said okay. Andrew brought out a big stack of Masters of the Universe comic books and fell in the armchair. Antoine played with his football video game. Argentina strapped on her headphones, flipped on her radio, and opened a magazine. I picked up Miz Imani's book.

It seemed like every minute was an hour long. After a while, Antoine and Andrew got hungry. Argentina got sleepy. I got antsy and couldn't sit still. "Let's call her now," I said.

"Yeah, it's been at least two hours already," said Antoine.

Andrew looked at the clock. "That clock must have stopped. It says it's only been about fifteen minutes."

Argentina called, but the line was busy, and stayed busy for the next two hours. "Who can she be talking to for so long?" Argentina said after trying for the tenth time to get through.

"Shuh, you talk longer than that," Andrew said. "C'mon, Antoine, let's go outside."

Argentina took the phone with her into our bedroom and closed the door. I flipped open Miz Imani's book to a picture of a Black lady with a thick brown fur around her shoulders. She wore sparkling earrings and a gold necklace. Under the picture it said, Madame C. J. Walker, First Black Woman Millionaire."

I read that she was born in 1867, the child of slaves. How could anybody Black have made that much money way back then? Miz Vereen said that our folks were all poor, digging in the dirt and picking cotton and tobacco until baseball and basketball came along.

I knew that rock stars and athletes were millionaires. Was this lady a rock star, too? Naw. The book said Madame Walker was a famous hairstylist, had her own hair and face cream business, and traveled all around the world. It said she got into hair because she had so many problems trying to get her own to grow and do what she wanted it to do. Wow! I wanted to read more about this lady.

Suddenly I realized that Miz Imani's book was easy to read because the words weren't hard. I liked the pictures, too. I read some more about this Miz Madame Walker. It said that she had a thirty-four-room mansion that looked like a palace. No wonder Miz Imani included her in this book about African kings and queens and heroes. I thought hard. Maybe I could be a hairstylist and a rock star, too.

But I even got tired of reading after a while. I pushed open our bedroom door and waved at Argentina until she looked at me. "Can I talk to Hattie?" I asked.

"She's not home. She and Maizell and their mom went somewhere."

"Well, could you call the hospital again?" I asked.

But when Argentina called, the line was busy. She called Raisin back and started to gossip some more. I sighed and lay back down on the couch. What a lonely ole day!

After a while Argentina came in. "Big

Momma's phone is still busy. Her Eastern Star sisters must be calling her." She sighed loud. "And I gotta stay home. C'mon, Mary Elouise, let's play Monopoly. Think the boys'll wanna play, too?"

I ran to the door and looked around for them. They were hanging off Deacon Rapture's fence in the back. "Get 'em, Malik!" Antoine hollered. "Bite 'em on the nose!"

Over in Deacon Rapture's yard was Deacon Rapture's dog, Malik, snarling and snapping and rolling on the ground with Bear, the big old fat brown dog from up the street.

"Stop, stop!" Miz Rapture ran out on her porch in her housedress and her plastic Jeri-curl cap. The dogs reared up on their hind legs, growling and biting at each other. They didn't pay a lick of attention to her.

Malik was part collie and part some kind of spaniel. He let me sit with him on top of his doghouse a lot in the summer. He wouldn't let Antoine or Andrew do that. He wouldn't even let the boys get in his yard. But neither would Miz Rapture. She said they tore up too much.

"Go, Malik! Chew 'em up!" Andrew shouted.

Miz Rapture grabbed up her water hose and turned it on the dogs. The spray smacked Bear in the face. It surprised him so much that he fell back on his haunches. Malik was all over him then! But Miz Rapture turned the spray on Malik, too. When the dogs broke apart Bear limped away dripping water everywhere. Woofing and fussing, Malik bounced stiff-legged after Bear.

"You better get your fuzzy tail back here," Miz Rapture yelled. Malik sat down, looking like he'd just won World War III. "And you boys get off that fence, for the thousandth time!"

Andrew was grinning. "But Mary Elouise, you shoulda seen the start of the fight. Ole Bear came up to Malik's water bowl and started to drink out of it. Malik was in his dog house. Man, Malik shot out of his dog house and onto Bear like a bullet!"

That was the most exciting thing that had happened all day, I thought. "You guys wanna play Monopoly?"

"Naw," said Antoine. "I wanna see if Bear comes back."

I went back inside. Argentina and I played hearts, and then spades. When the telephone rang, we both jumped up, but I got to it first.

"Hello, unh, Argentina? Argentina there?" said some boy.

Argentina sat back against the couch, studying her fingernails, and swinging her leg.

"And who may I ask is calling?" I tried to sound proper.

"Is this Mary Elouise?" said the boy. "Yo, Mary Elouise, this is Lamar. Put Argentina on."

"Is that Junebug? Or Big Head?" Argentina

whispered. "Lamar? Oh. Shoot. Say I'm not home."

"She's not home," I said, and hung up.

"You weren't supposed to hang up!" she screamed.

"What was I supposed to do?"

"Ask what he wanted. Take a message. Get his phone number."

The telephone rang again. "You answer it this time," I told her.

"No!" She shook her hands in the air. "It's Lamar again. Answer it, Mary Elouise, see what he wants and take his telephone number. Here's a pencil."

"Hello? What's your message?" I said. "What's your phone number? What do you want?"

"I want to see if you're all right," said Momma.

"Oh! Oh! Oh! Yes m'am. We're fine!" I stuttered, shocked.

"I been trying to call you all off and on for the last three hours. Is Argentina there? Good. Tell her to stay there. And to please keep off the phone. You okay? Everybody okay? Well, bye."

The telephone rang again.

I made Argentina take the next call.

"Oh hi, Lamar." She wound a strand of hair around her finger. "Babysitting," she said, looking at me.

"Babysitting who?" I pretended to frown up,

and put my hands on my hips, and tried to sound like her. Argentina stuck her tongue out at me and took the phone back into our room.

When Momma came home, Andrew and Antoine ran into the house, Argentina flew out of our room with the telephone, and I jumped up off the couch. We fell on her. "Momma—"

"I know what you're gonna ask. Yes, she's fine, she's fine," Momma said.

"Does she have tubes stuck in her?" Andrew wanted to know.

"Did they cut off her leg?" Antoine and I asked together.

"My goodness, you children've been worried something terrible," she said. "She looks the same way she looks at home in her own bed. She'll be able to leave Sunday morning. She's got a pretty room, and the nurses are nice. Shoot, when I stopped by after work she was sitting in the visitors' lounge with her legs crossed, talking with some of the other patients."

Momma told us that we would pick up Big Momma Sunday morning at the hospital and go to church from there. Then we'd bring her home here for a while before we took her on to Cuffy's Island.

"I thought it'd be better if she stayed here with us until Monday," Momma said, " 'cause it's getting colder and colder out there. But she said no, she wanted to go home."

We hurried around cleaning the house. Momma changed the sheets on her bed so Big Momma could rest if she wanted to. Then Argentina and Momma bustled around in the kitchen working on Sunday dinner while I tried to make the boys get their clothes ready for Sunday.

But Sunday morning came in freezing cold. I could see my breath in the air. Pulling my blankets around me, I sat up in our room. Momma and Argentina stood by our big old gas stove in the living room. "This darn thing," Momma said. "I was afraid the heat would go out when I heard the wind pick up early this morning. It swooped right down the pipe and blew out the pilot light. It's such a pain trying to light it back up. I wish I could get hold of the gas people."

"But it'll be warm in church," Argentina said. She hopped back across the wood floor and jumped into her bed.

Still wrapped in my blankets, I hobbled into the cold bathroom and washed quickly. Our house was colder this morning than it had been when the heat went out last month. I woke up Antoine and Andrew. They stuck their heads back under the blankets. After I flew back in our bedroom, I dressed quickly under my own blankets.

"Big Momma, be ready to check out of the hospital with all your belongings when we come," I heard Momma say on the telephone.

"What? You're ready now? You're really the early bird." Momma laughed. "We'll see you in a little bit. I'm going out to start the car right now. Our heat went out again. I think I can get it on again. Or I can bring out the little electric heaters. I sure wish I could afford a new stove this winter. Dress warm, hear? It's like a refrigerator outside. Yeah, this must be our ten cold days of winter starting. Okay. Bye."

Momma wrapped a scarf around her head over her pink curler cap and pulled on her boots. I wore my long brown winter dress coat, knit cap, mittens, my green sweater and skirt, and long green tights, but I was still shivering. "Big Momma'll sure be glad to get out of that hospital, won't she, Momma?" I asked.

"If that cold air flies up her dress she might not want to," Momma said back. She hurried out into the cold to warm up the car.

"You think it'll snow?" Andrew asked, huddled up beside me on the couch.

"Forget it, children," said Argentina. "There's not a cloud in the sky. I saw snow one time. It was fun for a while, but it got too cold for me. Snow is definitely not the big deal folks make it out to be."

It hardly ever snows down here. I hadn't ever seen snow in real life. I figured snow was like the ice on the freezer walls in our refrigerator. Or fifty thousand layers of frost.

Suddenly Antoine held up his hand to his ear. "Hey, how come I don't hear the car running?"

We scrambled to the window. I saw Momma's curler cap and scarf sticking out from under the hood of the car. I saw her get into the car. In a couple of minutes I saw her head under the hood again.

"Oh shoot, I bet it won't start!" Argentina said.

"If the car won't start, she won't be able to pick up Big Momma at the hospital," I said. We looked at each other.

After a few minutes, Momma hurried back inside. "I don't know what's wrong with that car, but it sure won't start," she said. "I'm gonna go back out after I warm up for a minute." She turned toward the stove. "Oh," she said. Her face went sad.

Momma sighed, picked up the telephone and sat down on the couch.

"Does that mean we can't get Big Momma?" I asked.

Momma turned around and frowned at me. "I got to get us squared away first. We can't get any-where right yet."

Momma called around for a repair man to fix the stove, but everybody was busy, or didn't an-swer. Then she called the hospital and told Big Momma the bad news. "Yes, when it rains, it pours," she said. "I'll keep trying to get them both fixed as soon as possible. Maybe we can still get you out today. I'm sorry."

She called gas stations and auto repair shops. They were either all busy or didn't answer, too.

Momma went back to the stove and got down on her hands and knees. The pilot light burner was way at the back of the stove and hard to reach. Momma hated to put her hand way back there with a lighted match. She was afraid she'd blow us up.

Plus, when it was windy, the wind would swoop down the pipe and blow out the match before she could get it lit. And sometimes the burner was even clogged up.

Disappointed, I slumped back on the couch. What next?

It took Momma all morning to find a tow truck to come out and try to start up the car. "M'am, either you need a new battery, or your starter's gone," the mechanic told her after he'd looked at the car. "I'll have to haul this baby in to the shop to fix her up. She won't be ready before tomorrow afternoon sometime."

Momma also asked him to look at the stove. He fiddled with it for a while, and finally got the pilot light relit. Heat! In a couple of hours the living room was warm enough for me to take off my coat.

After supper we talked to Big Momma on the

telephone. "I bet you feel awful still being in that hospital," I said, "when you could be at home, or with us."

"If I'd gone home today, my heat might have gone off tonight, with it so windy. I'd had to have been in that cold house all night. I wouldn't have minded being with you kids, but your heat might go off again. So I'm right here in this nice hospital, safe and warm. Everything has a purpose, see, baby?"

CHAPTER

THIRTEEN

We about froze walking to school Monday morning. My fingers felt like ice cubes. After we thawed out and school started, Miz Vereen took us to the cafeteria, where we rehearsed hard. At morning recess it was still so cold that the teachers kept us inside. Everybody played in their rooms, in the cafeteria, or in the hallways. It was loud and crowded everywhere. Hattie and I watched Miz Riley decorate the bulletin board by the music room.

"Miz Riley, how often are we gonna practice our play this week?" I asked.

"Lots and lots and lots." She pinned a black felt arrow onto a red felt heart. Then she stood back, frowning. We stood back and frowned with her. "I know!" She added black silhouettes of President Lincoln, President Washington, and Dr. King. That really perked up the bulletin board. All of a sudden I felt proud to see Dr. King's picture up there, too.

"Yeah, that's better," Hattie and I told her.

"Well, today's February 1," Miz Riley said. "Valentine's Month! Black History Month! President's Month! Friday's the big day for our play, you know. Let's see. We had a full rehearsal today. We will on Tuesday and on Wednesday, too. Thursday afternoon is the dress rehearsal. This afternoon, I'll meet with the chorus. Tomorrow afternoon I'll meet with the characters, and with you rappers, Hattie. Wednesday afternoon I'll meet with you narrators, Mary Elouise." She smiled at both of us. "Did you take your notes home to your folks?"

We nodded. "Momma said she was gonna come," Hattie said.

"Big Momma, my grandmother, is gonna come, too," I said. "Big Momma's in the hospital, but she's gonna come home today. Momma said she had to work, though."

"I heard she was in the hospital." Miz Riley stuck on pictures of Frederick Douglass, Martha Washington, and one of Harriet Tubman. "Oh, and, Mary Elouise, you've really done well with your part."

I grinned so hard I thought my lips would split. "Big Momma's been helping me. She took out some of the big words. Listen, Miz Riley." I stood real straight with my arms down at my sides. "Black people have a long, long history in America and in the world. This afternoon we are going to tell you about some famous Black Americans."

"She just heard you this morning," Hattie broke in. "Listen, Miz Riley—we're here to say that on this day a mighty man was born," she rapped. "We've been meeting, too, at the rec center. Me and her and Alicia and Kenyatta."

"Jermaine wanted to join in, but we said no boys," I said.

"No boys? C'mon, girls, let the poor things in!"

We laughed and shook our heads. I did kind of wish Jermaine could meet with us, though.

We hopped down the hall, rapping, and into our room. When Brandy came toward me with a pencil in her hand, I ducked my head and moved out of the way so she could get to the sharpener on the wall.

"Hey, Mary Elouise, you were totally awesome at rehearsal," she said.

"Hunh?" My mouth fell open.

"For sure. You knew all the words." She went to the wall and stuck her pencil into the sharpener.

Was I dreaming? Brandy spoke to me, for real this time, too. I sat down at my desk, in shock.

Miz Vereen told us to go outside after lunch because it was warmer. And guess what? While Hattie, Maizell, Timika, and I were hanging upside down on the monkey bars, Brandy came over to me again!

"That Miz Imani was cool, wasn't she?" she said. "Do you like her book?"

"Oh, unh, she is. I mean, it is. I mean, they both are." I remembered to tilt my head to one side. I wondered if I looked weird hanging upside down with my head slung over.

"Can I borrow it when you're done? I'll take good care of it."

"Oh, I'm, unh, I'm through now. I'll bring it tomorrow!"

"Fantastic. Thanks." Brandy smiled at me. "See ya."

I almost fell on my head climbing off the monkey bars. Everything was happening just like Big Momma said it would. See, here was Brandy, trying to be friends with me. I couldn't wait to tell Big Momma.

Brandy spoke to me that afternoon, too, right in front of everybody.

As soon as I got home, I called Big Momma's house, but I didn't get an answer. Was she still at the hospital? Had Momma got the car fixed? Maybe Momma hadn't picked her up, yet. I called over to the hospital. She answered on the first ring.

"Big Momma, how're you feeling? When you coming home? I got good news!"

"Well, baby, I got bad news. This ole doctor's not going to let me out today. Those silly tests came back saying something funny, so they have to give 'em to me again." She started to tell me what the tests were all about, but I broke in.

"Excuse me, Big Momma, but remember that girl Brandy I told you about? She talked and talked and talked to me today! She wants to borrow Miz Imani's book. Now we can go ahead and be best friends after all!"

Big Momma didn't say anything.

I waited until I couldn't stand it anymore. "That's my good news, see?"

"I see," Big Momma said. "Goodness, I sure wish these tests would get over with so I could go home."

"Big Momma, I been waiting all afternoon to tell you about my good news. Isn't it great?"

"Well, baby, I suppose it's good, if *you* think so. But I think you ought to just stay the same way with her that you've been doing lately."

"Oh. But why?"

"Because she sounds like such a moody kind of child, Mary Elouise. Say one thing one minute, say something else the next. I'm not so sure you ought to let her borrow that book, at least not yet. That woman wrote your name in the front of it.

Something like that doesn't come along every day. This Brandy child might not know the importance of that book to you. She might let something happen to it."

"It's just a book, Big Momma." I frowned. "It's not like this was something really, really important she was borrowing, like my mouse pin."

"Oh, I see. Well, sister, you go ahead and do what you want to do. I've tried to tell you. You can have such a hard head sometimes." Big Momma sounded like she was disgusted. "Say, that reminds me. Where's that Black doll I gave you for Christmas? I haven't seen you play with it since you got it."

I froze. "I . . . unh . . . oh, the doll? It, see, Big Momma, it got wet, and unh—" My voice trailed off.

Silence.

"Mary Elouise," Big Momma finally said, "you never did like Black dolls, did you? You'd always look so funny on Christmas morning after you opened up my box and found a Black doll instead of a white one in it."

I hunched up my shoulders. Had Momma told?

"I'd never thought about it until now," she said, "but those dolls, this girl, the play—it all fits together. You're color struck; that is, you're stuck on white and light. Baby, our color has had it so hard—"

"Oh, Big Momma, I get tired talking about that ole stuff all the time. This is different." I frowned hard.

"Your little hard-head side just showed itself once too often on this thing, Mary Elouise. I'm gonna tell you one more time, and then I don't want to have to tell you again. Hear me good, now! I'm gonna try to tell you nice and hope you hear. Otherwise somebody'll have to tell you and it won't sound so nice, and you'll be hurt and not know why. Just because somebody's white or Black and because somebody's got money or doesn't is not the way you choose your true friends. It's how they treat you that's the test."

She sighed heavily. "I'm tired, baby, and I don't feel like listening to this kind of foolishness today."

That hurt. "Well, it might not mean anything to you, but it does to me," I said.

Silence again. Geez, what did I say that for?

"Mary Elouise Avery, is that you talking to me like that?"

My face burned. "I'm sorry, I didn't mean it, honest," I mumbled. "I gotta do my homework. I gotta go. Bye."

"Good-bye."

I felt awful when I hung up the phone. I didn't ever want to say something mean to Big Momma. I hadn't wanted her to ever find out about the dolls, either. Would she be mad at me forever now? I just wished she could understand about Brandy, and how important it was for me to be friends with her.

But I had to stop on that, too. She was right, kinda, on why it was so important to me. Was it wrong to want to be around Brandy just because of who she was and what she had? My chin stuck out. Big Momma said it was. I still didn't think so, though.

When I picked up Miz Imani's book, I remembered that she had felt just like me one time. 'Course, she said she had changed. I looked at how she'd written my name in the book, and Hattie's, too. I thumbed through the pages. I was really proud of that book. It had helped me about how I felt toward Black History, I guess. Stuff didn't seem to be as embarrassing all the time. Her book, the play, and Big Momma helped, too. Maybe I *had* changed a little bit. I didn't want to change everything, though—at least not about Brandy.

Suddenly I grinned wide. Miz Imani's book would help Brandy and me be best friends! I imagined myself talking to Brandy on the telephone about the book, or maybe going to her house and us reading it together. Big Momma was wrong.

Tuesday morning I flew to school with Miz

Imani's book. I threw my coat up on the hook in the hallway, and rushed into the room, but Brandy wasn't there. I pulled the book out of my bag. Should I just drop it on her desk right now? Or wait and hand it to her?

Chaundra and Hattie came in. "Hey, I hollered for you and you kept running up the street," said Hattie.

"When, Hat?"

"Just now! What'd you have to get here so quick for?"

Brandy and Ashley walked in, laughing. My heart thumped. She came straight to my desk. "Oh, there's the book! Hi, Mary Elouise."

I almost jumped up from my desk, but I made myself take my time. I stood up and kind of poked the book at her. I put on my best smile.

Brandy began flipping through the pages as she walked back to her desk. "I'll bring it back and take good care of it."

Hattie punched me in the arm. "You're letting HER borrow that book?"

"Yeah. So?"

"So, I ain't even seen it all the way through yet, and it's half mine!" She stuck her hands on her hips and glared at me.

"Oh, cold!" Chaundra screamed. Everybody turned around. "Hat owns half the book and Mary Elouise turned the whole book over to Brandy!"

"Chaundra, shut up!" I hissed, embarrassed.

"Big deal." Hattie spun around on the heel of her hightop to make it squeak like someone breaking wind, and marched to her desk.

"Mary Elouise, you're cold-blooded," said Jamal.

"I don't care," said Hattie. "It's half hers, too. She can do what she wants to with it. I don't wanna even see it now."

My face was as hot as fire. Hattie! I hadn't even thought about asking her permission to let Brandy borrow it. But I didn't think she'd get so upset. I sat down with a thump, opened my spelling book, and held it up in front of my face.

But guess what? I saw Buffy and Ashley crowd in around Brandy during lunch recess—to look at my book! I stood by the turtle aquarium against the wall and watched them, waiting for them to say something to me. When they didn't, I wandered over and stood by them. Finally I asked, "How do you like my book?"

"Fine," Brandy said as she turned the pages. "Ashley, there's that Queen Nefertiti."

I tried to think of something else to say, but I couldn't. They didn't say anything else to me. I walked back to the aquarium, leaned against the wall, and watched.

After school, Brandy, Ashley, and Buffy walked up to me. "Mary Elouise, do you mind if I take your book home and show it to my parents?" said Brandy.

"Oh, sure! Yeah." I nodded eagerly.

She turned around and headed for the door. Grabbing my book bag and coat, I hurried after them. Kids poured out of their classrooms and streamed through the doors to the outside. I pushed through, too, to keep up with Brandy, who stood by the curb with the other girls.

"Did you see Miz Imani's name on the cover? Isn't she like, wow, just totally awesome?" I said. "Maybe I could go home with you today and we could read it together."

Ashley and Buffy giggled. Brandy's ears turned red. "Mary Elouise," she said, "I don't think you can—"

"There's your mom." Ashley tugged on Brandy's arm. She and Buffy pulled her backwards away from me.

"I could show you stuff in it on the way home," I hollered after her. "Or maybe I'll just call ya, okay? Bye!" I waved and waved as Miz Howard's Mercedes pulled away.

I couldn't believe it. I talked to Brandy, with Ashley and Buffy there, too. Maybe I could ask her if she wanted to study together, instead. Ashley and Buffy could be there, too, if she wanted. I wouldn't mind.

When I turned around, I saw Lonnie Lee and

Bonnie Boo looking at me. I kind of lifted my chin. "I was talking with Brandy and Ashley and Buffy," I said.

"Omigod, like totally awesome, you know!" Lonnie Lee hit a pose with her fingers in her hair, imitating Brandy. "She is such a snob. Silly, couldn't you tell that she didn't want you to come over to her house? Alicia Valendez and Kimiko think she's snobby, too. I heard Brandy say she'd die if she ever had to eat grits for breakfast. You got to be snobby if you don't like grits, right?"

"Gotta be," said Bonnie Boo.

I shrugged. "I bet she eats steak and stuff like that."

"I don't know what you see in her, Mary Elouise. She only likes people who are rich and live in condos. She only likes to be around certain people."

I frowned. Lonnie Lee was just jealous.

I walked home by myself. I didn't see Hattie, but I wasn't looking for her, either.

I wanted to call Big Momma when I got home, but I was ashamed after the way I'd talked to her yesterday. That night Momma said Big Momma was doing all right and wanted to leave the hospital, but that they were still running tests. I hoped she could still come to the play.

Wednesday went by fast. I heard Brandy tell

somebody that Kenyatta had the flu. During math class, while Miz Vereen's back was turned, I asked Brandy if her folks liked the book. She said they thought it was very nice. When I asked her if I could eat with her, she said maybe, maybe on Thursday.

I was so surprised that I about jumped in the air. "Okay, okay, okay!" was all I could think of.

But Lonnie Lee poked me in the arm with her pencil eraser. "You're the stupidest thing I ever saw," she snapped. "That girl don't want to be bothered with you. She thinks you're weird."

"Sure does," said Bonnie Boo.

"Mind your own business," I snapped back.

Lonnie Lee's mouth went O-shaped. Then her cheeks turned red. She stuck her chin in the air and went back to working on her math.

I floated in the air all day. Lunch with Brandy! On the way home from school I saw Hattie and Timika on the other side of the street, but they didn't speak to me. I didn't care. Brandy was my friend now, and soon we'd be best friends!

When I got home, Momma was already there. "I went by the hospital and took Big Momma some magazines. She said you hadn't talked with her since Monday."

I didn't say anything, and Momma didn't ask me anything more. Deep inside I wanted to call Big

Momma badly, to try to explain and apologize. I wanted to see if she was all right, too. But I didn't I guess I still was too ashamed.

On Thursday at dress rehearsal I think we did pretty good—all but Jermaine. Afterward, I saw Miz Riley take him to one side and sit him down beside her on the piano bench.

Kenyatta was back today, too. When she smiled at me in our room, I smiled back wide. I wanted to tell her that Brandy and I were tight now, too, but I didn't. I figured she'd find out herself. I hoped she didn't get mad.

Just before lunch Hattie bumped into me and almost knocked me over in the hall, but I didn't do anything back. I just went right on into our room, and headed for Brandy's desk. I was eating with Brandy today.

I fingered my mouse pin. I took a deep breath. "Ready? I'm like, totally hungry."

"What?" She stared at me. "Oh, I'm eating with Kenyatta," she said. She leaned back toward Kenyatta.

"But you said—"

"Yeah, but that was when she was sick and gone. She's back now."

"Oh. Well, can I sit on the other side?"

"Buffy's sitting there."

I tried to keep from frowning. "Well, can I sit across from you, Brandy?"

"Brandy said I could sit there today," said Ashley, who was listening.

"But you promised me, Brandy." I could feel my shoulders start to droop.

"Mary Elouise, it's just lunch, you know." Brandy twisted her head to one side and rolled her eyes at me.

I used to think that made her look cute, but today it made her look stupid. "I gotta have my book back," I told her, "right now." I could feel tears coming, but I definitely would not let anybody see me cry today. I just wanted to get my book and get away from her desk.

"Okay. I brought it back. Listen, Kenyatta wants to see it. I was gonna show it to her at lunch. You don't mind, do you?"

But that part burned me up. I stamped my foot. "No! It's my book! Give it here, right now!"

Brandy lifted up her desk top, pulled out my book, and handed it to me. The jacket cover was stiff and wrinkled like it had got wet and then dried out. Some of the pages were stuck together. I opened it up to the page where Miz Imani had written our names. The ink was so badly smeared that I could barely read Hattie's name. I couldn't read mine at all.

"What happened?" I cried out.

"I dropped it in my bathtub. Sorry. I didn't mean to. But I have tons of books at home so look,

I'll give you one of mine. It's signed by the person who wrote it, too. Course, it says Brandy, but you can scratch out my name and put yours in it."

"No, that's tacky, Brandy," Kenyatta said.

I just stared at the blobs of ink streaked across the page. I pressed my lips together, and tears jumped into my eyes.

Hattie came over to us. "You said you what with our book, Brandy? I know you didn't say you messed up our book, did you? Because I don't want any of *your* ole books. I want ours."

I clumped back to my seat, and, trying not to cry, lay my head down on my arms. Boy, I felt like an old tin can out in the woods, rusty and dirty and thrown away. Was I ever dumb about Brandy. She really didn't understand how important that book was to me. She didn't even care! She had bunches of books at home. Our one little book didn't mean anything to her. And she didn't keep any of her promises. Big Momma was still right, all the way. Brandy was back to being the way toward me that she'd been before. She couldn't ever be my best friend. And now I didn't want her to be.

"C'mon, Kenyatta, lunch," I heard Brandy say.

"I'm eating with Yolanda today," said Kenyatta. "You ought to buy those guys a new book of Miz Imani, Brandy."

Brandy shrugged. "Yeah, sure. Ashley and I'll come sit with you and Yolanda, okay, Kenyatta?"

"No," said Kenyatta. "We're sitting with Timika and Hattie and Lonnie Lee and Bonnie Boo. And Mary Elouise."

For a minute or two all I heard were footsteps going out the door. I kept my head down.

"Hey, Mary Elouise, you okay? Hey, maybe if we talk with Miz Nisby or Miz Vereen, they can get Miz Imani to sign another book. What do you think of that idea? Hey, you gonna eat with me and Lonnie Lee and Kenyatta and them?"

That was old Hattie. She put her hand on my arm and shook it a little.

"C'mon, Mary Elouise, they're waiting on us!" That was Lonnie Lee.

I glanced up. My eyes felt puffy. Lonnie Lee smiled at me a little. Kenyatta, Yolanda, and Timika stood in the doorway waiting. Hattie looked at me and shrugged. "C'mon, girl," she said. "I'm hungry. We'll get us another book just like that. C'mon. I ain't mad at you anymore."

That's when I knew who my real friends were. I nodded my head, whispered "okay," and wiped my eyes.

CHAPTER

FOURTEEN

Time for the play!

I jumped out of bed early Friday morning and hurried across the cold floor to get into the bathroom before Argentina or the boys did.

As I brushed my teeth, I sent up a prayer to the Lord for me to do everything right this afternoon. I wanted Big Momma and Momma to be proud of me. I started to tap my foot in time to Hattie's rap, and to hum the words.

Suddenly Mary Inside reminded me of something—You were silly to be chasing after Brandy, and now everybody knows it. People are gonna call you color struck.

I remembered yesterday, and my face burned. No, Brandy didn't care anything about me. The way she'd handled Miz Imani's book proved that. And I was stupid for the way I'd been trying so hard to make her my friend, for all the wrong reasons, just like Big Momma had said.

I also realized that Lonnie and Bonnie Boo, Timika and Alicia—even Kenyatta—were my true friends. And my best friend was still Hattie.

"And they still like me," I said into the mirror. "And I'm not ever going to try to get somebody to be my friend just because they're rich, or white, or 'cause I think they're better than me."

I told myself I wasn't going to be color struck anymore about wanting light skin either—but I bet that was going to be a lot harder. Momma was always talking about who was dark-skinned and who was light-skinned and who was pretty and who wasn't. We all talked about stuff like that and were always comparing.

When I came out of the bathroom, Momma motioned me over to the couch. "Let me comb your hair."

"I know every single word of my speech, forwards and backwards," I told her. "And I know where I'm supposed to stand on stage. And I gotta talk loud, but not too fast."

"You're just as ready as you can be. You sure sounded good when you said your speech for me last night. I'm mighty proud, Mary Elouise."

I grinned, and my face got hot with pride. She brushed my hair back tightly, snapped a rubber band around it, and wound white baubles around my ponytail.

"Big Momma said for you to wear these." She held out the ivory hair combs. "And I said you could wear these of mine. Don't you dare lose these, hear?" In her other hand were her tiny ivory earrings.

My mouth fell open, then I hugged her hard. "Oh, Momma, thank you! I promise I won't even shake my head, not an inch. And when I see Big Momma this afternoon, I'm gonna hug her hard and thank her, too."

I also planned to tell her again I was sorry about being sassy with her. I was going to tell her that I was finished forever with Brandy. I was going to tell her that she had helped me out a lot about not getting embarrassed or ashamed every time something came up about Black people.

"Mary Elouise, listen." Momma paused. "I got bad news. Big Momma won't be able to come to your play."

My heart went flat. "Can't come? But she said she'd be there! She promised she would!"

"She's still in the hospital, remember? Her doctor's not done with her. Plus, it wouldn't be good for her to be out in this cold air. She's so sorry,

Mary Elouise. She wants to talk to you. Have you talked to her lately?"

I hung my head. "No, m'am. I was going to last night, but I forgot."

"Well, why don't you call her right now and thank her for the combs. She misses you badly."

I rushed to the telephone and dialed. What was I going to do? Big Momma couldn't come.

"Hey, Namesake, good morning," said Big Momma. "Your momma told you, did she? This thing hurts me like the dickens, not being able to come to your play."

"Big Momma, I'm gonna be so scared without you there," I said. "What if I mess up again?"

"Baby, you won't mess up. After me coaching you along, showing you how to do? You just remember me, you hear? Just imagine I'm sitting in that audience, listening to every word. 'Cause I won't be able to be around you all the time in this world. But I just want you to remember how to do, and you can. If you put your mind to it, you can do it. Don't be afraid. Listen here—you can carry your Big Momma around with you in your heart wherever you go, all the time, no matter what happens."

That sounded so sad that I started to cry on the telephone. Momma came over and sat down beside me. She put her arm around my shoulder.

When I was able to talk, I told her about the

Black dolls and what I had done. "I'll never mess them up again, Big Momma, I promise."

"Oh, that's no worry about that. You're getting too big for dolls now anyway. It's your ideas behind it that you gotta work on. You ain't by yourself having color-struck problems, baby. Most everybody in this world got 'em in one way or another. I just hope what I told you and what you learned about all those wonderful Black folks you're gonna be speechifying about will help you have some pride about who you are."

"Yes m'am."

"And when you got pride about who you are, you can step with the best, no matter what color your skin is," she said. "Course, I'm kinda partial to the color yours is right now."

"You gotta get to school or else you'll be late," Momma told me.

"I gotta go, Big Momma," I said, "but I'll call you just as soon as I get home and I'll tell you everything that happened, okay? Bye."

"It's not fair," I said to Momma. "Nobody's gonna see me from home."

"Ain't fair for neither one of us, Mary Elouise. Argentina said she'd try to come. Baby, I'm sorry. We'd sure like to have been there."

She slid the combs in my hair and her earrings in my ears. "There. That really perks up your hair. Now straighten up your face. Don't you get up on that stage this afternoon looking like that. We may not be there in person, but you know we'll be thinking about you." She patted my cheek. "We'll be wishing you the best, honey."

I looked at her through my swollen eyes. "Yes, m'am. I'm gonna try to do my best."

But how? Big Momma wouldn't be there. Momma wouldn't, either! How could I do it?

I dragged myself out the door and into the chilly air. Hattie and Maizell were waiting for me at the corner. When I got to them, Hattie asked me what was wrong. I told her. She didn't say anything. She and Maizell hooked their arms through mine. We walked up the street to school.

I tried hard to concentrate on my lessons, but the butterflies in my stomach wouldn't let me. At recess I stayed inside so I wouldn't get dirty. Plus, I didn't want to lose the combs or earrings.

"Cheer up," Hattie said. She wore white leotards, a short blue skirt, and a red blouse. She looked like a flag. "You gotta do your thing for the other folks who come, remember?"

"Yeah." Well, that was a thought. It wouldn't be the same, though.

Lunchtime flew by, and the next thing I knew, it was time for the play. The kids who had character parts were dressed in old-time costumes. Brandy wore her long, blue Martha Washington dress with a white apron, white bonnet, and a white shawl. Miz Vereen had stuck her long, blonde hair up under the bonnet. She wore lipstick and rouge, too.

When we lined up, I found myself standing right beside her. "Mary Elouise, I'm sorry about your book," she said.

At first I wasn't going to say anything, but Mary Inside got the better of me, so I did. "I'd never borrow stuff from people I didn't like," I said.

"I like you," she said.

"What?"

"I liked you enough to borrow your book."

"But not enough to do anything else, hunh."

She just looked at me. "Mom's gonna get you a new book and Miz Vereen's gonna give it to Miz Imani. She said Miz Imani is still here, visiting down on Turner's Isle. You know, you DO act weird and geeky when you mess with my hair and follow me around. Maybe if you weren't so weird—" She trailed off, slouched her head to one side and smiled at me.

Listening to her, I wondered something. Did she mean then if I stopped doing that stuff she'd be my friend?

Naaaawwww, said Mary Inside. Too little, too late, sister!

Miz Vereen switched past. "Quiet, quiet, no talking in line," she said. "Now we must walk quietly through the hallway to the rooms of the teachers in charge of your parts, remember? Characters, you go to Miz Cutterhorn's room. Chorus and rappers, you go to Miz Riley's. Mary Elouise and Black History people, you go to Miz Thomas. From there file quietly into the cafeteria. Remember to walk with your feet and not with your lips."

"How can anybody walk with their lips?" Lonnie Lee whispered to me. "They'd trip!"

"Where'd you get the pretty combs and earrings?" Hattie whispered just before we split up to go to the different rooms.

When I told her, she said, "See, you got that part of them with you. Lots of kids don't have nothing or nobody here. I'm scared. Are you?"

"Yeah. Miz Riley let me carry these little cards with my speech written on them just in case I forget."

Miz Thomas lined me up with the other kids in the Black History section, then marched us into the cafeteria, where the play was being held. Suddenly I saw all these faces and eyes watching us. My heart thumped hard. There were Hattie's and Yolanda's mommas. There was Pooch's grandmother in the back row. There was Libby's aunt Miz Eva Dell. Lucky! I glanced around the big room, hoping for a miracle, but I didn't see Momma or Big Momma. I didn't even see Argentina. I sighed and sat down.

Remembering what Hattie said, I touched the combs and earrings. That helped a little.

The cafeteria quickly filled with the rest of the school kids, and us fourth-graders. Aaron and Kasheba must have been baking inside those dog and cat suits. Cupid wore his red and white Cupid outfit. I saw him stick his sponge arrow into the ear of the boy beside him. Then the lights dimmed.

Miz T came out from behind the curtains and stood at the edge of the stage. She wore a long green, yellow, and red robe like one Miz Imani had worn. "Ladies and gentlemen, parents and student, thank you for coming to our annual Presidents' Month program. You are in for a treat this afternoon. Our fourth-graders have worked especially hard to present to you an excellent program."

As Miz T talked, Miz Cutterhorn motioned to the characters to follow her through the door leading to the side entrance of the stage. "We will feature a Valentine's skit, a Presidents' Month segment, and a new addition, a Black History segment," Miz T went on. "We'll have music galore and a special Bicentennial rap. So sit back and enjoy. Thank you."

In a few minutes George Dozier came out on stage, dressed in blue pants, a white shirt, and his red bow tie. He was as stiff as a soldier, with his shoulders squared back and his fingers pointing hard at the floor.

"America can be proud of its noble achievements," he began. George Washington marched in with his white wig on crooked. Everybody laughed and clapped.

Ben Franklin got a little confused over what he had discovered. He said he had discovered a key instead of electricity. But Martha Washington didn't miss a beat.

Kimiko Johnson came out in a white dress with red and blue trim. Her long black hair was tied back with a red ribbon. "Roses are red, violets are blue. This Valentine's play is just for you," she began.

In the Valentine's skit Aaron the dog was supposed to very gently push the girl who played the ball of yarn over to Kasheba, the kitten. But Aaron banged into the ball of yarn like he was a football player, and sent the ball spinning into the kitten. The ball knocked the kitten down, then rolled over her. Miz Riley had to come out on stage and set the ball and the kitten back on the right track. I laughed so hard my side hurt. But then I remembered that my turn was coming up fast. That shut me up, and I got scared again.

When the curtains opened next, the rappers came strutting out to the edge of the stage in their white leotards, red shirts, blue pants and skirts, and red baseball caps on backwards. There were twenty of them stretched out from one end of the stage to the other. Hattie and Timika were right in the middle.

We're here to say
That on this day
A Mighty Man was Born.

And on this date
We'll celebrate!
Everybody come blow your horns!

Then they did a little dance, kicking and stamping their feet, and throwing their arms left and right, in time to the music. They looked good! I knew Hattie had got some help from Maizell, since Hattie couldn't dance a lick.

Somebody hollered out, "Get it, girls and boys!"

When Miz Vereen whispered to us that it was time for the Black History segment my knees started to shake. We followed her to the back of the stage. I fingered the combs again. Big Momma and Momma, I'm gonna pretend you're in the audience, and I'm gonna talk real loud, I said inside. I told myself not to look into the audience. Maybe that way I wouldn't be so scared.

I saw Jermaine hunched up against the wall by the fire extinguisher. He was crying! I went over to him. "Hey, why you gotta do this now? It won't be that bad."

"Yes, it will. I can't do it," he said. "It's too hard."

"Yes, you can. Just take your time."

Kenyatta came over too. "You can do it. Just remember what Dr. King said about letting there be peace in heaven and a place on earth for every race, or something like that."

"That's not what he said," Jermaine said, and gave her the correct quote.

"See, you do know what to say!" She threw us her big, dimply smile. "Good luck, Mary Elouise."

"Thanks. Good luck to you, too. Kenyatta, I gotta ask you something, okay?" I cleared my throat. "Are you best friends with Brandy now? I mean, I don't care, but I was just curious."

Kenyatta laughed. "My best friend's still Yolanda. Brandy's okay, but she's kinda weird sometimes, you know? She's been trying to be best friends with me for the longest. Maybe when she's not so sometimey and weird I might be best friends."

I couldn't help but laugh when she told me that. I wanted to tell her I wanted to be better—not best—friends with her, and that I was sorry for acting so stupid. But I didn't. I just stuck out my hand, and she shook it.

"My best friend is Hattie," I said instead.

"I know. Hattie's cool."

"Mary Elouise, come to your spot," said Miz Vereen.

I hurried over to the center edge of the stage

behind the curtain. Miz Vereen took my hands in hers, and patted them. "Do the best you can, my little sugar dumpling," she said. "I know you can do it. You've come a long way. You don't know how proud of you I am."

I wanted to hug Miz Vereen when she told me that. Instead I touched the combs and earrings. The curtains started to move. I took a deep breath.

I felt very small standing in front of so many people. The lights were very bright. A cold flash of air across the stage sent goose pimples up and down my arms. Suddenly I had to go to the bathroom. What was I supposed to say? I glanced down at my cards. They weren't in the right order. I squeezed my eyes shut tightly. No tears, no tears this time, please!

"You can do it if you put your mind to it," I heard Big Momma's voice say just as clear as a bell inside my head. "Now tell me your part, and start at the start."

I opened my eyes and took a deep breath. "Black people have had a long, proud history in America and in the world," I began. I pulled myself straight and squared my shoulders. "This afternoon we are going to tell you about some of our many famous Black Americans." I moved a little off to the side. "Here is Kenyatta Threadgill, portraying Sojourner Truth."

Right on schedule, Kenyatta whipped around

the corner and stood where I had. She was dressed in a long gray dress and a bonnet. Her cornrow braids hung down around her shoulders. She was perfect in her speech. Everybody applauded. Next was Joey Hollenstein as Frederick Douglass. He stumbled over a couple of words, but got back on the right track quickly. Yolanda McCray as Harriet Tubman was dressed the same as Kenyatta. She didn't wear a rag on her head, or runover shoes, either. Alicia Valendez as Marian Anderson did all right, too. So did Pooch as Alexander Morgan G. Dickson. In fact, he was better than Miss Jamaica In-Charge.

For an instant I let myself glance down into the audience and I got the shock of my life. Right there, right in the front row, were Miz Imani and Mr. Kwanzaa. When she saw me looking at her, she smiled and held up two fingers in a V-for-victory sign. Don't you know that really made me stand up straight and grin!

I clumped back out to the middle of the stage. "And now, the humble Baptist preacher who showed the world that nonviolence was the way to peace. We all say thank you, Dr. Martin Luther King, Jr., for what you have done to help set all people free," I said.

Jermaine came out. I could see his legs shaking. His hands were clasped tightly behind his back, clutching his notes. "I have a dream," he began. "I . . . I . . . I have a dream."

As he recited Dr. King's famous speech, he stumbled over some of the big, long words. His voice began to tremble. Once he got confused and couldn't say anything. He started again, and tripped over some more words. He'd tremble and slow down, then pick up again.

Then I realized that he was crying. But he didn't stop trying to give his speech. And he wouldn't look at his notes. His words were just clear enough to be understood, clear and trembly at the same time.

"Take your time, son," someone said in the audience. "Teach us. You're doing fine."

Jermaine paused and wiped his eyes with the back of his hand. The audience began to applaud, and kept applauding even when he started again. At the end of the speech, Jermaine was shouting. I guess he was afraid people couldn't hear him over the clapping. That set folks to clapping even harder.

When he had finished, everybody in the cafeteria gave him a standing ovation. Jermaine was confused. He was supposed to lead all of us off the stage, but he just stood there. People kept clapping, too. Finally Miz Riley motioned to me to come off stage, so I did, and everybody followed me, including Jermaine. People still clapped.

"You kids are just marvelous!" Miz Riley whispered. "Now go finish up, Mary Elouise." She pushed me back out.

"That is the end of our Black History segment, but this is not the end of our history," I said. "We have come a long, long way, and we still have a long, long way to go. We can all be proud of our achievements as—as African-American people. Thank you."

When I slipped back behind the curtains, Miz Thomas was there. "Wonderful, honey." She hugged me. "Oh, you were just darling!" she said. "I'm so glad you decided to keep the part. That's why I wanted you to do it, to bring you out of your shyness. I knew you could do it!"

"Miz Thomas, you made a beautiful choice." There was Miz Imani. She bent down and hugged me, too. "You were wonderful!" She smelled like Christmas spices. She handed me a package. "Another book—but this time just for you. I'm going to give Hattie her own, too."

"Big Momma couldn't come because she's still in the hospital," I said.

"I understand," said Miz Imani. "But I'm here."

"I'm glad you are, too." Suddenly I got shy with all this attention. We stood for a second listening to the chorus singing "Somewhere Over the Rainbow." Then I peered up at Miz Imani. She was so pretty. "Can I ask you something kinda personal? Are you real famous and do you travel all over the world?"

"I don't know about famous, but I do travel a lot."

I thought hard. "Can a person be a rock star and a hairdresser and a writer and a storyteller, too? 'Cause I wanna be just like you, Miz Imani."

"Sure, you can. You can be anything you want if you put your mind to it," she said.

I handed her the book back. "Will you hold this for me until the program is over? I don't want to lose it."

She said she would. "And did you write the same thing in the book, about us being royal queens?" I asked.

She nodded again. Then she kissed me on the cheek. "Keep up the good work. You're making all of us so proud."

With the other kids I hurried back on stage for the finale. I was so excited I could barely breathe. Wait until Big Momma hears about this!

ABOUT THE AUTHOR

ELEANORA E. TATE, a native of Canton, Missouri, has written professionally for over twenty years. Her first book about children, *Just an Overnight Guest,* became the basis for a film produced by Phoenix Films, Inc. The film was named to the "Selected Films for Young Adults 1985" list by the Young Adult Committee of the American Library Association.

Ms. Tate's second book about children, *The Secret of Gumbo Grove,* takes place in the same town as *Thank You, Dr. Martin Luther King, Jr.!,* and was named a 1987 Parent's Choice Gold Seal award winner. *The Secret of Gumbo Grove* is also available in a Yearling edition.

The author is a member of the Association of Black Storytellers and the South Carolina Academy of Authors. She is married to photographer Zack E. Hamlett III, and lives in Myrtle Beach, South Carolina.